A Home in the Sky

Other titles from INDIAN WRITING

Krishna Krishna by Indira Parthasarathy

Star-Crossed by Ashokamitran

I, Ramaseshan by Aadhavan

Love and Loss by Jayakanthan

Wings in the Void by Indira Parthasarathy

Once an Actress by Jayakanthan

Bridges by Sivasankari

A Home in the Sky

Aakasa Veedugal

Vaasanthi

Translated from Tamil by
Gomathi Narayanan

INDIAN WRITING

A Home in the Sky
A novel in Tamil by Vaasanthi
Translated by Gomathi Narayanan

Pages 240, Price Rs 200

INDIAN WRITING - 5

ISBN 978-81-8368-351-7

An INDIAN WRITING publication
Published in India by New Horizon Media (P) Limited
33/15, Eldams Road
Chennai 600 018, India
Phone: +91-44-4200-9601/03/04
Fax: +91-44-4300-9701
Email: indianwriting@nhm.in
Website: www.nhm.in

First published in Tamil in 1981
INDIAN WRITING translation first published in 2007

About the author

Vaasanthi, former editor of *India Today's* Tamil edition, has authored thirty novels, six short story collections, two volumes of journalistic articles and four travelogues. As a novelist and journalist, she has been a champion of human rights, gender issues, and communal harmony. She has won many awards for her writings, which have been translated into various Indian and European languages.

This work, *Aakasa Veedugal*, has been translated into Hindi and Czech.

About the translator

Gomathi Narayanan has taught in Kerala and New Delhi. Her articles and translations from Tamil literary materials have appeared in *Indian Literature* (Sahitya Akademi) and other periodicals. She has translated Ashokamitran's *Padinettavathu Atchakodu* (*The Eighteenth Parallel*, Orient Longman) and *Iruvar* (*Sand and Other Stories*, Orient Longman). She has also translated with Lakshmi Holmstrom, Sundara Ramaswami's *Waves* (East-West Books), published later in *Sura: That's It But* (Katha Publications).

Gomathi Narayanan's published works include *The Sahibs and The Natives*, (Chanakya Publications, Delhi) a comparative study of British and Indian fiction. She has translated Vaasanthi's short stories *Kutravali—The Guilty and Other Stories*—(Indialog Publications, New Delhi).

CHAPTER ONE

First came the dots. The white spots falling on the wet earth. Blob after blob of chalk powder dropping from Lalita's nimble fingers. She was bent over the ground, drawing the morning kolam at the frontyard. As her hand flew swiftly above, below and around the framework of dots, lotus petals opened out on the ground. Creepers climbed and coiled. And parrots perched on them—a composition in white, adorning the front yard.

'What a fine artist you are, manni!' said Meenu, who had been watching the kolam take shape. She was sitting on the platform in the porch, her feet swinging merrily. On her feet she wore slender silver anklets above a border of bright red. She had hennaed her feet the previous night. Lalita felt like fondling each single toe of those fair soft feet.

The girl said something just now, didn't she?

'What's it, Meenu?'

'What lovely kolam patterns you draw! You're quite an artist.'

Lalita laughed away the compliment and went on adding a few finishing touches to the parrot's feathers. Then she looked up.

'How do you manage to be the way you are, manni?'

'What way is that?'

'Forever smiling, forever active, forever busy with housework.'

Lalita laughed again, patting her fondly on the cheek.

'But my dear girl, when you have a house, you are bound to have housework. If I don't do it, who'll do it for me?'

'I can't remember another person who smiles through her chores.'

'What's all that chattering out there so early in the morning? Will I get my coffee today?'

Lalita picked up the bowl of kolam powder in a flash and hurried in.

Sabhesan had dipped his fingers in sacred ash and was drawing it across his bare chest in swift strokes. The speed with which he was doing it was an indicator of his temper.

'My, has he had his bath already?' wondered Lalita with a pang of guilt for having lingered at decorating the front yard. She hurried to the kitchen. 'Just a minute, please,' she said.

'There's no discipline in this house. No sense of what to do and when.'

Lalita silently brought his coffee to the large swing in the hall. Sabhesan drank it and plonked the empty tumbler and dabara on the swing, loudly signalling again that his anger had not abated.

Meenu peeped in to make sure that her mama had had his coffee, and then came in. 'Mama, do come out and have a look at manni's kolam', she said. 'Do you know what a lovely pattern she's drawn there?'

'Just the sort of thing that's always happening in this house. A kolam is meant to be just a few lines drawn for form's sake. Spending hours at the front yard and wasting half a can of kolam powder! At this rate, this house is never going to prosper. Never!'

Sabhesan pulled out a shirt from the clothesline, put it on in a hurry, thrust his feet into a pair of worn-out slippers and stomped across the patch of earth in front of the house. Meenu stood aghast watching his merciless feet scuff out the kolam decoration. As the parrots and lotuses blurred and mingled with the dust, her eyes dimmed with tears.

'Meenu!'

Meenu went in hurriedly. 'Yes, manni.'

'Won't you have your coffee?'

'Coming!'

Meenu drank her coffee silently and ventured a question. 'Does mama always behave this way?'

Lalita's face betrayed no emotion.

'How does he behave?'

'Peevish and cantankerous, all the time.'

Lalita laughed. 'It's just that temperaments differ. A few minutes ago you were surprised that I could laugh. And now you are surprised that your mama could get angry!'

Lines of thought appeared on Meenu's face. Lalita pretended not to notice the change and went on putting some lentil to cook on the earthen firewood stove. Then she began to cut some okra.

'Shall I chop it up, manni?'

'Sure you can chop without cutting your fingers?'

'Of course!'

'Must wake up Raju', mumbled Lalita as she went to an inner room.

Raju was fast asleep. Even in sleep the boy's face wore a look of utter helplessness and fear. As always, Lalita felt a surge of anxiety at the sight of that face—a choking in her heart, a wetness in her eyes.

'Raju!'

Raju woke with a start and sat up, blinking and bewildered.

'Get up dear, it's quite late.'

'But I feel so sleepy!'

'Go pour some water on your face and eyes. That'll drive the sleep away. Come on, get up, now.'

He stood up, asking her softly, 'Amma, is Father in?'

'No. He's left for the fields.'

Lalita could almost feel his muscles relax instantly. The strained look on his face vanished. As sadness overwhelmed her, she wondered, 'Why is this hardened heart of mine still troubled every time I look at him?' Calming herself she went into the kitchen, where Meenu was chopping the vegetable, her head bent in apparent concentration.

This girl has a sharp mind. And sharper eyes, thought Lalita. She was here for just a month's holiday away from the city. How much could she observe? And how much deduce? Will she be disturbed by all that goes on here?

'Manni, why don't you get a pressure cooker?'

'Those things won't go well with firewood stoves, Meenu'

'Can't you get kerosene in this village?'

'We can.'

'Then why do you want to smoke to death struggling with this firewood stove?'

Lalita laughed out loud at her mention of death.

'Meenu, look at me properly and tell me if you have seen anyone with a stronger grip on life!'

Meenu looked at her with a brief smile and continued chopping.

The girl is wiser than her years, thought Lalita, as she mixed coffee and milk for Raju.

'I'm really surprised, manni!'

Lalita was amused. 'Oh dear, not again? What's it this time?'

'You know, we have a gas stove, running water, a fridge and a whole lot of things in Madras. Still, mother's grumbling all the time about something or other. Sometimes, when the gas is used up and a new cylinder does not arrive in time, we have to cook on a kerosene stove. You must see the fuss mother makes on those days! We all wish and pray for gas, gas, gas, every one of us!'

Lalita smiled to herself at the thought of Meenu's mother, Bala. The tempestuous Bala, Sabhesan's sister, with her sudden laughter and the stormy scenes she created, was really and truly Sabhesan's sister. Until Bala was married off, Lalita used to wonder how such a girl was ever going to adjust to a husband and run a home. Her worries were over, however, when Bala's husband, Saminathan, turned out to be her exact opposite. He never raised his voice, never asked questions, never wanted Bala to account for her expenses. A finely balanced couple indeed!

The thought would have made her smile, but then a few tiny cracks pushed though her armour. If only Sabhesan had been like Saminathan! His voice never raised in anger or abuse, his conversation not about money and accounts. Oh, what a lovely home this would be!

Then, perhaps, the kolam drawn at dawn would remain undisturbed till the evening. A few tiny dreams could then have flowered. A fifteen-year old girl would not have been shocked into asking, 'Is mama always like this?' An eight-year-old's eyes would not wake up in the morning with a hunted look, and the implied question: 'Is father in?'

Mere wishes, idle wishes! She dragged herself back to the present. Raju had not yet had his coffee. She hurried to the well behind the house.

Raju was there, seated on the washing-stone, watching a squirrel scampering up and down the coconut tree.

'Raju!'

He turned round with a start. Sorry that she had called him so loudly, Lalita added, in a subdued voice, 'Brush your teeth, dear, and come in and have your coffee.'

'Coming!' he said, but did not move. She stood there, looking at his back for a few seconds. This boy should have been born elsewhere, or at least, born tough enough to stand up to his father. But he had been born here, half-witted and with a petal-soft heart. What had the future in store for him? Sabhesan's favourite remark was: 'This boy is my retribution, my karma catching up with me.' What sort of man would Raju grow up into, hearing that, day in and day out?

'Do brush your teeth and come in Raju!'

Seeing him get up, she turned and saw a man's figure at the doorstep.

'Who's it?' Lalita asked softly.

'It's me,' said Balu Vadyar, a teacher at the municipal school. He was carrying his son Krishnan on his shoulder.

'What's the matter? Is Krishnan not well?'

'He's had high fever since last night. I am going to fetch the doctor from the town. Can I leave him with you till then, please?'

'By all means. I'll look after him'.

Lalita quickly spread a blanket on the bench in the hall and brought a pillow. Balu Vadyar laid his son down on the bench, and stood hesitantly by. 'Hope it's no trouble', he murmured.

'Certainly not.'

She was afraid to say more, lest the man burst into tears. She felt sorry for him when he thanked her and went out.

'Who's that, manni?'

'A teacher in our school.'

'Has he no one else at home?'

'No.'

'What about the boy's mother?'

Raju came in with a tumbler of coffee and said, 'That boy's mother has run away.'

'Hush! Raju!' Even as Lalita spoke the words, the tumbler fell from Raju's hand. But it was not in response to her rebuke, she sensed.

For, standing in the doorway was—Sabhesan.

CHAPTER TWO

For a moment Lalita stood confused, unable to react. The foolish stare on her son's terror-struck face gave her a sinking feeling.

Sabhesan came straight to where Raju was standing. The boy cowered. Sabhesan sprang at him and caught him by his hair.

'Don't hit him!' Lalita cried.

'Get away from here, woman!'

Sabhesan began to shower blows on his son.

'You wretch! Standing here, gossiping with women! Say you won't gossip again! Say you won't! Say it!'

'I won't. Please don't beat me! I won't gossip. Oh, it hurts!'

'Say it again. I won't gossip'

'I won't gossip! I won't gossip'

Meenu stood stunned. Lalita's eyes filled with tears. Sabhesan took it all in, but shouted as if he had noticed nothing. 'Go in, all of you! The way you are bringing up the boy! At this rate, this house can never prosper. Never!'

Without a word Lalita went into the kitchen. Meenu went to the next room.

'Get up, you good-for-nothing! Mop up the coffee you spilt on the floor and then go sit down and say your multiplication tables.' Raju brought the mopping-cloth from the backyard and wiped the mess on the floor. Lalita saw from the kitchen that his back still shook with sobs. The poor child hadn't drunk even a sip of coffee. She badly wanted to make some more for him but suppressed the desire by force of habit. When Raju went back to wash the cloth, she could hear the maid, Lakshmi, saying softly to him, 'No, Let me wash it. You go back.'

When Raju passed the kitchen on his way to the hall, Lalita, unable to control herself any longer, whispered, 'Would you like some coffee?'

Raju hesitated, his eyes betraying a fleeting temptation.

'No!' he said firmly, in control of himself again.

'Well then, go and say your tables without any mistakes, darling!'

'Okay.'

He began in a voice gruff with crying.

'Two ones are two...'

Lalita found it hard to concentrate on her cooking, worried that Raju would make mistakes. Soon, however, she remembered that Sabhesan would be preparing for his daily prayers, and began to make the arrangements, moving about like an automaton.

'Four fours are sixteen…'

'Hey, you!' shouted Sabhesan, 'Just look at these puja utensils! Didn't you scrub the panchapatra and uddharani with tamarind?'

'But, I did!' replied Lalita.

'Is this the way to wash them? Look at the grime.'

'Eight fours are thirty two...'

'You needn't wash the puja-things any more. I'll do it myself.'

'I'll try to wash them brighter.'

'No, you need not!'

'Five fives are twenty five…'

Sabhesan went to the kitchen in a huff, took some tamarind from a jar, went to the well, rubbed the copper puja-bowl and spoon with it, washed them clean with water and came back. Lalita stood by helplessly. The sight of his scowling face made her wonder now, as always, 'Oh God! Won't that face ever look pleasant? Some day… perhaps?'

He began the puja loudly ringing the bell and chanting.

'Suklambaradharam Vishnum

Sasivarnam chaturbhujam

(Meditate upon Him, the omnipresent,

The four armed one,

His radiance that of the moon,

His attire white,

His face graciously benign,

He shall help us overcome

Every obstacle in life!)

Lalita was now even able to laugh silently. 'Does he know the meaning of those words, I wonder!'

'Four sixes are twenty...'

Oh!

Tense with apprehension, she went quickly up to Raju in the hall and prompted him in a whisper, 'Say it right, Raju!'

'Four sixes are twenty...'

'Twenty-four, dear!' she whispered.

'He's been saying those tables day after day, every day, for two years now, but can't say them properly yet! What am I to make of this boy?'

Startled, she turned round. There stood Sabhesan, features contorted by fury, hand upraised.

Lalita blocked his way.

'Please don't beat him. It was only a slip. He has to bathe and leave for school now.'

'Get away from here! This woman is forever butting in to plead for that boy. As if he is the future collector! Now! Say it again—'Four sixes are?'

Raju stared blankly at his enraged father, forgetting the little he knew.

'Four sixes are...'

'Say it right! Or else, I'll skin you alive!'

Before Sabhesan could reach him, Raju began to cry.

At that moment somebody called Sabhesan, 'Sami!'

Sabhesan dropped his hand and looked through the window at the figure outside.

'Who's that?'

'Me, Sir, Pavadai.'

'I see. What's it about?'

Sabhesan went to the front porch after telling Raju to have a quick bath and leave for school.

Raju's face cleared in a second. There was even the trace of a smile on it when he looked at Lalita. Seeing him hurry towards the well for his bath, she murmured, 'May that Pavadai live long!' Pavadai was likely to stay for half an hour; time enough for Raju to get ready and leave for school. She breathed again.

After his bath, Raju daubed his forehead with some holy ash and, with eyes closed, prostrated himself on the floor in prayer before the pictures of the gods. Watching him go through his routine as if he were just repeating a lesson, Lalita was deeply affected.

Eight years old! Gopali next door is also just eight years old. But look at the way he talks and boasts! And the things he knows! All this, though born of illiterate parents!

'Can I have my rice, amma?'

'Yes. Sit down.'

Thoughtfully, Lalita watched him. He had forgotten all that thrashing and abuse and was eating his food with relish. Lalita felt that he might have been cleverer than Gopali if he had been born in the next house. There would have been more light for him, more air to breathe, too. He would flash a grin like Gopali. He would be rid of that blank stare. He would not make silly mistakes in the tables he'd been repeating daily for two years now.

'Give me some more curry...'

He would not have been so passive, so insensitive.

Pavadai was discussing something seriously with Sabhesan when Raju left for school.

'Then I'll start early tomorrow, after worshipping Panaiyatha', said Pavadai.

'Yes. That's right. You can go now.'

When he came in, Sabhesan was deep in thought.

'Serve my food,' he commanded.

She served him quickly. He ate in silence and got up. Putting on a shirt hurriedly, he said 'I'll be late in the evening. There's a lot of work to be done. By the way where has Balu gone leaving this child with you?'

'To fetch the doctor.'

'You seem to have agreed to look after him without even finding out about his illness.'

After a moment's hesitation, Lalita replied: 'It's only for a short while.'

'No wonder your son is what he is. You are such a busybody.'

Lalita bit her lip. He was deliberately working himself up into a frenzy. She felt weary.

Tucking his umbrella under his arm, Sabhesan said, 'When Balu comes, ask him to take back his son. I don't want you making a fuss over that child.'

'All right.'

Lalita followed him with a long vacant stare as he climbed down the front steps and went out. She closed the door after him and came up to Krishnan who was lying limp on the bench in the hall. She placed her palm on his brow. Krishnan opened his eyes.

'Shall I get you some coffee, Krishnan?'

'Yes', he nodded.

The boy's high fever and the pathetic look on his face troubled her.

'When will Appa be back?'

'Quite soon. Let me bring you your coffee.'

As she mixed some milk and coffee, she thought again of the boy's yearning, orphaned look and felt uncomfortable.

How could that woman leave such a child?

'She's run away!'

How was it that even the slow-witted Raju knew those words?

The way he said it, as if it were an ordinary everyday affair, without realising what it was really about, seemed to indicate that it must be a commonplace among the children of the village. How cruelly he had been punished for uttering those words in all innocence! To what purpose, when the boy could not know why he was being thrashed?

Krishnan drank the coffee. Then, suddenly he began to cry. Stroking his back, Lalita said, 'Don't cry Krishnan. Your father will be here any moment.' But she was disturbed. She tried to comfort him but he kept sobbing till at last, exhausted, he lay down on his side facing the wall.

There was a knock at the front door. She opened it. It was Balu, back with the doctor.

'How is he?'

'He was asleep all this while; I gave him some coffee just now.'

The doctor examined Krishnan. From the stock of medicines he had brought with him he chose what was required and left it with them.

When the doctor had left, Balu lifted Krishnan up.

'I'll take him home. Thank you so much,' he said.

'Can I make some rice-gruel for him?'

'No. You've already been kinder than I deserve—looking after him for so long.'

At the doorway he stood and spoke again haltingly, 'I wouldn't have asked anyone else so freely for help.'

'You must never hesitate to ask us.'

She was able to sense the looks darted at him through the windows of all the houses in the neighbourhood, as he walked homewards.

Finding Meenu standing in the hall, she smiled and asked, 'Won't you come and have your meal now, Meenu?'

Meenu refused with a brief 'Uhum...'

'But why?'

'It's just that I'm not in the right mood.'

Lalita laughed.

'Come. I'll set it right. Is your mood such a wilful thing that it smiles one moment and scowls the next?'

Meenu stood looking through the window in silence. After a while she said hesitantly, 'How many of us can be like you?'

'Talking about me again? Come let's do something useful. The food is getting cold and you know we don't have any gas here to warm it up again.'

'I was so shocked by the way mama thrashed Raju. I won't be able to eat for two days thinking of it.'

'Then don't think of it!'

Meenu looked at her with a tinge of wonder. Then she said, fixing her gaze on the street, 'Don't misunderstand me manni, but your acting as if nothing has happened, is even worse than mama's anger. It seems so unnatural.'

Lalita was startled by this remark but managing a smile, she said, 'What do you want me to do? Start shouting like him?'

'Can't you at least show him that you object? You needn't shout.'

'How? And in any case, when I know it's absolutely useless, why should I object?'

'If I had a husband like that I'd just run away!'

'It's easy to talk Meenu.'

'Why did she leave her husband?'

'Who?'

'That boy's mother.'

'I don't know!'

'That's not true. You're just afraid mama will get angry.'

'Not exactly. Why should we bother ourselves about all this? In any case, everyone will give you a different reason. Only the woman concerned knows the real reason.'

'Where's she now?'

'In town.'

'With whom?'

'Some man or other.'

'Oh!'

Lalita laughed. 'Meenu, are you just sixteen years old or sixty-one?'

'I'll try to be sixteen. Give me some curry!'

'So you've come round at last!'

When they had finished eating, they found the maid, Lakshmi, waiting, obviously wanting to say something.

'What is it Lakshmi?'

'Amma, do you know why Pavadai came this morning?'

'No!'

'Didn't Sami tell you?'

'No!'

'It seems that Sankaralinga Iyer is going to sell away his land.'

'And then? Where'll his meals come from?'

Lakshmi laughed. 'It seems he has a son employed in Madras. All of them can go there.'

'What! The whole lot of them!'

Lakshmi laughed again: 'He must be tired of his village mistress and village drinks.'

'Lakshmi, you talk too much! I oughtn't to have spoken to you at all!'

'All I wanted to tell you was that our Sami is going to bid for that land.'

'Quite possible,' Lalita said with a vague resentment gnawing at her heart. 'I'm an outsider in this house.'

There was a knock at the back door. A woman was standing in the backyard. Lalita was astonished to see her there.

CHAPTER THREE

'Who's that, manni?' inquired Meenu.

Lalita whispered, 'Krishnan's mother.'

'Rukmini-Amma is here!' announced Lakshmi.

Lalita went up to her, smiling.

'Come in. Why do you stand out there?'

Rukmini stood there, irresolute, troubled eyes surveying the scene. There were fine lines beneath her eyes and at the corners of the mouth.

'No Lalita. I'd rather not come in. Let me sit here on this platform.'

'Well then, let's sit here.'

Rukmini sat down, embarrassed and hesitant. Lalita sat down facing her.

'Who is that in the house? Someone I don't know?'

'That's Meenu, my sister-in-law's daughter, come from Madras for the holidays.'

'I see,' Rukmini sat looking down, evidently groping for words. Feeling sorry for his plight, Lalita began, 'What is it, mami?'

'Krishnan's ill, isn't he?'

'Yes, but how did you find out?'

'The town-doctor's daughter told me. I just couldn't stay away after hearing that. The heart has no reason. I caught the first bus, and here I am.' Rukmini was blushing. Beads of sweat stood out on her forehead.

Lalita looked at her in surprise. It was hard to believe that this woman had so resolutely severed all ties with her family. She thought of a similar scene two years ago.

'Better hang oneself than live this kind of life. I'm still putting up with everything, only for my son's sake', Rukmini had said then.

But she neither put up with things nor hanged herself. Instead, she left her husband. The village hadn't yet ceased to condemn her act. They said she was with some Chettiar in town. Her husband, Balu, the teacher, does not walk erect any longer.

It was shocking to see this tired woman who had come all that way in the hot sun because—as she said—her heart wouldn't listen to reason.

'How is Krishnan?' asked Rukmini. 'Lakshmi told me he was left with you.'

'He did have rather a high fever. The doctor examined him and has given some medicines. He'll be all right, don't worry.'

Rukmini buried her head between her knees and began to sob.

How does one pacify her? She was not weeping because of the boy's illness. It was something else, something that the boy had wept for earlier that morning.

The maid Lakshmi, busy washing the utensils, was watching her, amused. Lalita said, 'Mami, don't cry!'

Rukmini looked up wiping her tears with the end of her sari. Then she got up and went to the well, drew some water and washed her face.

'Mami, come in and have some coffee.'

From Rukmini's face it was obvious that she was grateful for the kindness.

'Let me sit in the hall', she said tearfully, 'I won't enter your kitchen.'

Lalita brought her coffee in silence.

As she took the tumbler of coffee, she said, now openly crying: 'You're different, Lalita. I wouldn't be allowed to enter any other house in this village.'

Lalita chose to overlook the remark and said with a smile, 'So, how are you mami?'

'Is that a query about this body of mine? Why, it's okay. Shamelessly okay. I mean, three meals a day, good clothes to wear, a bed to sleep on and all that.'

What sort of things would she come out with next, wondered Lalita and squirmed.

'It's a curious thing, Lalita. When you don't get enough to eat, food seems the only thing that matters. But once you're full, you are disgusted with your body. I wonder if you can quite understand what I say.'

'Yes – I can.'

'No, you can't. Only those who have gone through it all can understand me. My sufferings were real, and this was the only way I knew to end them.'

Lalita wished she would leave without saying anything more. Meenu must be listening to this talk.

'There never was enough to eat. There wouldn't be a single grain of rice to cook in my house for half the month. The man drank and gambled away what little he earned. No one here bothered about my children and me. And no one bothered to tell him, 'It's not proper for you, a school teacher to behave like this.' That's because he is a man! But when I could bear it no longer and left, the village cursed me as 'the woman who ran away.' If I had stuck to this place, do you think this Brahmin street would have fed me?'

Lalita was touched by the sorrow and anger of the words so plainly spoken. Rukmini wiped her tears, looked at her and continued, 'Only those who have gone hungry can understand the misery of hunger. My husband used to give me some money—but hardly enough to last a week. What was I to do for the rest of the month? Sometimes I used to wish I'd been born in the non-Brahmin quarter of this village. For there you can do any kind of work to earn a living. But as a teacher's wife in this Brahmin quarter, I was helpless. I tried to get a job as a cook with some family in town. I tried really hard—but I could get no work. What else could I have done?'

Lalita lowered her gaze, thinking, 'But I didn't ask you to explain your actions, did I?'

'And now, Lalita, I'm not begging, cheating or robbing. All I'm doing is using this body of mine which belongs to me after all.'

Lalita did not dare to look up. She shrank from the matter-of-factness of Rukmini's tone.

'Lalita, believe it or not, I have begun to feel detached from my body. This is just a dress. It can be put on and pulled off, just like that. My dress has become soiled in this birth, so what? I can atone for everything in my next birth. I have nothing to do with this body of mine.'

Lalita felt like laughing out loud. What an odd philosophy! Doesn't she realise that once the clamour of hunger has been stilled, the clamour of love will be heard? And the body she has nothing to do with has come running in the sun to visit her sick child!

'The only thing I can't forget is my love for my son,' Rukmini continued. 'I tried to keep him with me! But the people, the accursed people of this village, turned him against me. He used to love me so!'

Lalita thought of the boy's weeping, his face turned to the wall. Then she looked at the time-lined, tearful face of the mother and wanted to say: 'You could have avoided all this, if only you had clenched your teeth tighter and held on a bit longer.' But she didn't say it.

'Manni' – It was Meenu calling her.

'Yes, Meenu!'

'Lakshmi wants something. Can't quite make out if it is green-gram or...'

'Oh, I'd asked her to clean the green-gram dal. Wait, I'm coming.'

Upon seeing Lalita, Lakshmi whispered, 'Amma! How long are you going to entertain that woman?'

'Poor woman! Leave her alone.'

'You pity everyone. If Sami comes to know of this, we'll see who is really to be pitied!'

Lalita felt her heart miss a beat. How was it that she had forgotten her own plight? She gave Lakshmi the dal in a winnowing pan and returned to the hall, where she found Rukmini gazing at the sky through the window.

How can one turn away a woman who had come all that way in the sun craving sympathy and understanding?

Rukmini stood up.

'Let me leave now. I will send somebody tomorrow or the day after to find out about Krishnan. Please let me know.'

'Yes, of course, I'll let you know.'

About to leave, Rukmini stopped as if she had just remembered something, 'How are you, Lalita?'

'Oh, fine! Can't you see?'

'And your husband's temper and tantrums?'

Lalita laughed. Rukmini stood looking at her thoughtfully for a moment, then said, 'In the eyes of men, women are no better than pack-animals. No better than those bullocks that go round and round, yoked to the oil-press in the village. But just you wait, you men! The bullocks are raring to bolt and break free! And when that happens...!'

Lalita felt a tremor traversing her frame. She stood stunned, watching Rukmini stride up to the back door, open it, and go out.

'Wow! What a rousing dialogue!' exclaimed Meenu when Rukmini had left.

'Well, she lives in town and probably goes to the movies quite often!'

Meenu laughed aloud, 'But she does have a point there, hasn't she?'

Lalita wondered if Meenu wasn't too young to make such a remark.

'What do you feel about it, manni?' Meenu insisted.

'Well, I can't say. There must be some very valid reason for everybody's actions. After all, one acts in a particular way, only because at that moment, it seems the right thing to do.'

'But do you think she did the right thing?'

'I don't know. But she feels the need to justify it to herself.'

'She's a great feminist, manni. If only we had four women like her in every street, we could put down all these hectoring men.'

Lalita didn't reply. She thought, 'Every street will then be swarming with orphans!'

Lakshmi was busy cleaning the green-gram, muttering to herself: 'You a Brahmin woman, falling so low, how could you expect any respect in this village?'

Lalita lay down on the long plank of the swing, a pillow under her head. Through the window she could see a patch of light blue sky with floating clusters of white clouds. She looked at the changing patterns made by the clouds – small dwellings and tall palaces – all up there in pure white, beyond the reach of the ugliness, anger, disappointments and cravings of the earth down below. If only our minds could soar that high! From those dizzy heights, our mundane affairs would look so trivial that our hearts would be freed of anger, carping, irritation.

This ego, this 'I' or 'me' would not then benumb our mind and turn us into beasts. There would be no need then, to repudiate the body, or treat it like an alien commodity.

But why is it that the mind does not ever fly and soar? Well, how can it, when it's imprisoned within the high walls of the ego!

This 'I'—

This 'I' can blind us to feelings of honour and shame. It can make us blind to love. It can make someone furious at an eight-year old's hapless remark, or a mistake in his sums, or his slightest act of carelessness. But who is there brave enough to deal this ego a deathblow?

'Just you wait... The bullocks are raring to bolt…' What if they do bolt and break free?

What then? Only that the animal will be dubbed a 'runaway' and a 'good-for-nothing'?

CHAPTER FOUR

There was a large portia tree in the backyard besides banana, lime and coconut trees. Meenu amused herself watching the tiny sparrows flit from tree to tree.

Standing beneath the lime tree, she felt a coolness pervade her body, from the soils of her feet to her eyelids. It was incredible that it could be so cool here. The slate-paved courtyard behind her had been so hot under the scorching sun that she had had to cross it at a run to reach the shade.

'This village looks beautiful, once you get out of the house', she thought.

She climbed on to the washing-stone under the shade of the spreading branches of the portia tree and looked round. Beyond the few rows of houses, everything was green, parrot green. The village lay surrounded by this green velvet, shimmering in the sun.

Amongst these green fields, if people don't get enough to feed themselves, it isn't the fault of the land! She thought of Rukmini's lament that morning. 'What else could I do when I had nothing to eat?'

Could it be that Rukmini said things like that just to convince herself?

'Whatever happened, there was absolutely nothing wrong in her leaving her husband. I'd have done so myself,' Meenu told herself.

After all, if a husband gambles and drinks away what he earns and lets his wife go hungry, what else can she do but leave him? And what's so wrong about it?

In any case, that Rukmini mami is quite an interesting character. Those who break rules are always interesting.

But look at people like Lalita manni! They are bound to be treated worse than animals turning the oil-mill. And quite rightly so! In the three days that Meenu had spent here, she had found her manni silently putting up, again and again, with her husband's outbursts of temper. Every time she saw her do that, she had felt tempted to go to her, shake her and say, 'Be natural! Protest! Show him that you too have feelings!'

But, if manni does protest, how will mama react? Will he beat her till she cries herself hoarse, as he does with Raju?

'No, I-won't-gossip! I-won't-gossip.'

Meenu covered her eyes with her palms as if to shut out the scene she had visualised. Her fingers trembled.

Was he human, this uncle of hers?

He seemed to derive some pleasure from his cruelty. Born elsewhere, he would have been a Mafia leader. Did he consider Lalita and Raju his bond-slaves? Or could it be that they considered themselves bonded to him? Why else did Raju look and sound so perpetually terrified?

How different her manni was from her mother! In Madras, her father's voice was seldom heard at home. Mother's was always the dominant voice. One had to see this mama to recognise what a gentleman father was. Mother must come and stay here a couple of days. She'd learn to appreciate father.

'What are you doing here, Meenu?'

Lalita was standing with a hand on the backyard door.

Those eyebrows, that nose and that pale gold skin. Her Lalita manni was beautiful! Could her mama be blind to this?

Lalita came up smiling.

'Didn't I ask you what you were doing here?'

'Nothing! It's so cool here, manni. From the top of this stone, the whole village looks green! And what a lovely place it is!'

Lalita sat down on the washing-stone with a faint smile.

'But if you stayed here, you'd hardly notice the greenery, Meenu! Will you go in now and bring me a small bowl for the jasmine? There are such a lot of buds on the bush today! Let's pluck them!'

'Leave them on the bush today, manni. We can pluck them tomorrow.'

Lalita took her head in her hands and looked at her thoughtfully for an instant. Then, with a slight smile she said, 'You think too deeply for your age, Meenu. Those who ponder deeply suffer deeply. Look at me! I don't spend any time on reflection and analysis. I just let each minute's experience die with that minute.'

Meenu laughed, 'I don't believe you!'

'Think what you like. But really, I have no grievances.'

Meenu felt it would be impudent to dispute such an assertion.

'I believe,' Lalita went on, 'that no wrong deed is done on purpose. It's just that people's ignorance and foolishness lead them to do wrong. If we magnify this foolishness and grieve over it, we are being all the more foolish.'

'Well then, there's no need for law-courts or the police, in this world of yours!'

Lalita sat looking at the birds hopping from branch to branch on the portia tree.

'It does seem like that, Meenu', she said softly, 'If people love one another, there's no need for the police. It's only because we have so completely forgotten what 'love' means, that we suffer so.'

Meenu laughed. 'You're good at spiritual discourse. Maybe you'll make a good teacher!'

Lalita got up. 'Do you know what your mama will say to that, Meenu? 'Let me first see you wash the panchapatra and uddharani bright. And then, do the talking!' That's what he'd say.

Meenu's face tightened.

Lalita patted her lightly on her cheek. 'Why do you take small things so seriously? Let me make you some coffee. Meanwhile, pluck all the jasmine buds. We can make some garlands for the holy images.'

Plucking jasmine buds, Meenu wondered how it was

possible for a woman to be like Lalita. She seemed proof against anger or pride. Was it possible never to harbour any ill feelings, never to be angry? Or was this mere play-acting? And if so, how long could one pretend?

Meenu pulled herself up and chided herself for indulging in pointless speculation. That look on Lalita's face! That smile of hers! How could they ever be put on? Why should she play-act? Who was she out to deceive?

Perhaps herself?

No. Such self-deception would have bred bitterness and hate. Those feelings would have slipped out in her conversation. She would not then have been so kind to everyone. She would not then have shown such kindness to a woman who had been ostracised by the rest of the village, nor entertained her in the central hall of her house.

According to Lalita, everyone suffered because they had forgotten what 'love' meant. Love must be a rare commodity, indeed. That was why she, Meenu, could not understand her manni.

When she went in with the jasmine buds, the evening coffee was ready. They drank their coffee and sat down on the platform in the porch to string the flowers.

'Meenu, what are you going to do now that you've finished school?'

'I want to join college and work for a degree. Women have to be educated, if they want to be free. Otherwise...'

'Otherwise?'

'Well, these men will just crush us beneath their heels!'

Lalita burst out laughing. 'So you think education is your weapon in your war on men?'

'We don't need education as a weapon. We need it to

toughen our own characters, to strengthen our own wills!'

Lalita laid the jasmine down. She caressed Meenu's cheeks tenderly with both hands. 'How smart and intelligent you are, my girl! Go ahead! Study well, widen your horizons, then act. But act, to build. Never to destroy.'

'I am not out to destroy anything manni. Don't you worry! Look there! Is that Raju back from school?'

'Why, Raju, why are you back so soon?'

'Classes are over!'

'What's the matter?'

'Seems like they're showing some good film in town today. The teachers have all gone to see it.'

'What's this, manni? Can it be true?'

'Well, that's the way our school is run. During the harvest season, half the students are busy in the fields and don't attend school. If a few do show up, they'd say, 'Who can teach for the sake of one or two children?' And so the school would be closed.'

'Why have you put Raju in such a school, manni?'

'This is the only school we have.'

'Why don't you bring him to Madras? He won't learn anything here.'

Lalita laughed. 'A lot of people have left for the city for some reason or other. That's why this place is going to ruin. If we leave the place, there'll be no one to look after our lands.'

Meenu thought of the boy's helplessness and his vacant stare and decided that he was not fit for higher education. It would be foolish to expect much from him.

Then something caught their attention. It was a black

Ambassador driving past the house raising a cloud of dust. It stopped in front of a house three doors ahead.

'Whose house is that, manni?'

'The previous owner has sold it and left for the city. This may be the new owner.'

By now women and children from all the houses on the street had come out to watch the car and its occupants with unconcealed curiosity.

Meenu was embarrassed. 'Come manni, let's go in', she said.

A tall light-skinned man, in a modern outfit got out of the driver's seat, took off his dark glasses and looked about him with obvious interest.

Meenu stood up hurriedly, collecting the strings of jasmine and the leftover buds. As she stood up, she hit herself against the low roof and bent down, massaging her head. She found the newcomer watching her with a look of amused sympathy.

CHAPTER FIVE

When she woke the next morning, Meenu felt a pain at the top of her head, right at the middle of the parting of her hair. She stretched lazily and felt the bulge, then thought of the newcomer. His whole personality and dress seemed to be out of tune with the village.

She had to shake herself free of all thought of the stranger with a firm reminder: 'What does it have to do with me, if someone chooses to come to this place?'

Her mama was bathing at the well in the backyard. He seemed to do everything with deliberate seriousness. Every little thing must be done according to plan, every single happening fill up the mould that he had cast for it. In his preoccupation with little things, was he perhaps allowing big things to slip through his fingers?

Her manni was right, thought Meenu. She did have a tendency to analyse everything. She brushed her teeth and then went into the kitchen.

Lalita was already busy.

'I've left your coffee here, Meenu.'

'I've slept too long, manni. Why didn't you wake me up earlier?'

'What's wrong with getting up a bit late? After all, you're on a holiday here, aren't you?'

Meenu gulped down her coffee, as if she had urgent work to do.

'Can I chop the vegetables up for you?'

'Yes. Cut this snake-gourd. I'll get things ready for mama's puja.'

'Nobody need do anything for me! I can get all my stuff myself!'

When Meenu looked up with a start, there he was with a scowl on his face!

Oh God! What has made him lose his temper now, so early in the morning? Meenu watched, as her mama stomped about leaving imprints of his wet feet on the floor. She saw him hurrying to the well with the panchapatra, uddharani and the big plate. Lalita followed him, walking hurriedly, yet softly – 'Give me the vessels. Let me wash them.'

'No, you need not!'

Lalita drew back, as if whiplashed.

The upright blade of the chopping plank cut Meenu's trembling finger. When Lalita came to the kitchen, having left the betel leaves, betel nuts and bananas at the puja alcove, she found Meenu holding up her finger, blood dripping.

'Oh Meenu! Get up, wash your hand and twist a wet cloth round it. I'll chop the vegetables.'

Meenu got up, waited for her mama to leave the well and then went to wash her hand.

When she came to the porch, she found Raju, slate on lap, watching the street.

'What are you doing here, Raju?' – She had spoken the words quite softly. Yet Raju gave a start.

Sorry for the boy, she sat next to him and looked at the sums on his slate. 'Why don't you do your sums, Raju?'

'I'll do them now.'

He looked at his slate, but did not seem to see anything.

'Who gave you these sums?'

'Father.'

She felt her stomach turn in fear. Was he in for another beating?

'Shall I teach you how to do them?'

'Yes, please.'

There was a sheepish grin on his face. His imbecile look hovered somewhere beyond her.

'Look at my hand. It's all here. You've got to add two more.'

She spread out her fingers.

'Now, what comes after five? Six. Write it down...Good! There! You've done it well!'

Raju's face brightened at once.

'Now, what's two plus two, Raju?'

Raju blinked.

'Look at my hand again. You've got two here – Now after two... What's the next number?'

'Three, then four!'

'Good, write it down.'

Fortunately, Sabhesan was still at his puja when Raju finished his sums. Raju looked at Meenu. He placed a hand lightly on her thigh and asked, 'Meenu akka! Will you teach me arithmetic everyday? I seem to follow it well when you teach me.'

Meenu, still doubtful about how far he had really grasped his arithmetic, agreed gladly and said, smiling, 'Now go and show your sums to your father. He's finished his puja.'

He went in, wearing a proud smile.

When Meenu got up, she bumped herself again on the head, just as she had the day before.

'What! Yesterday's bump forgotten so soon?'

Meenu looked up with a start, still nursing the top of her head. There he stood, the young man who had arrived in his Ambassador the previous evening. He flashed a fine set of teeth under his dark moustache.

Unable to decide whether his remarks were friendly or impudent, she blushed uncomfortably.

He continued, 'Sorry. I didn't mean to tease you. That question, I assure you, was asked with genuine sympathy!'

'Thank you!' she said but without returning his smile. 'I won't ever sit on this porch again.'

'But why be annoyed with the porch? It happens to be the only place of entertainment in this place!'

Now she smiled in spite of herself and countered, 'But there are so many other ways of killing time!'

Sabhesan's voice was heard from somewhere inside the house. It acted as a timely reminder that her mama would not like her talking to a stranger. Who knows, he may even beat me like Raju if he finds me here, she thought with mock seriousness.

But as she turned to go in, the stranger said, 'Don't people usually inquire of a visitor what he wants or whom he wants to meet?'

Meenu stopped to look at him. There was light-hearted mockery in his dark eyes.

'Sorry. Whom do you want to meet?'

'Is Mr. Sabhesan in?'

'Yes. I'll let him know. Please sit down.'

'I'd rather not sit down. You see, I'm quite as forgetful as you!'

She couldn't help laughing.

When she reached the hall, she found a tearful Raju facing his scowling father. But all his sums were correct, wondered Meenu.

'Mama, somebody has come to see you.'

Sabhesan put on his mask at once, the knitted eyebrows straightened; the face relaxed its severity.

'Who is it?' he asked, as he made to go to the front.

'I don't know. He's out there in the porch.'

It was surprising how she had learnt to adapt her answers to her mama's tastes in just three days!

Raju was hastily wiping his tears away.

'Why Raju, your sums were all correct, weren't they?'

'But he was cross with me for writing my six like a zero.'

'Doesn't matter. Just write it better next time.'

'I will.'

But she thought, 'No, he won't.' His mind is not going to develop. Today's fear and sorrow will be tomorrow's anger and hatred.

'Meenu!'

She turned quickly.

'Ask manni to make a tumbler of coffee and bring it here.'

'Yes mama.'

Meenu was surprised at her mama's hospitality. Why was it that his face and demeanour underwent a transformation the moment he set eyes on Lalita manni or Raju?

'Manni, mama wants you to make a tumbler of coffee.'

'Who's the caller?'

'The man who came in his Ambassador yesterday.'

When the coffee was ready, Meenu took it to the porch and called her mama. The visitor looked up, and hearing her voice, smiled in recognition. Meenu was afraid that her mama might notice it. She went in without returning the smile.

The man sat talking with her mama for nearly half an hour. She wondered how he could talk to this scowling mama for so long. She even thought that the scowl on Sabhesan's face had relaxed slightly in the course of their conversation. Raju avoided Sabhesan and managed to eat and leave for school without making the least noise. When he smeared the sacred ash on his forehead and prostrated himself before the images of the gods, she found herself wondering what the poor boy would be praying for—a better disposition for his father perhaps!

After her mama had left for the fields, she sat on the platform in the backyard. Lakshmi was washing vessels at the well.

'Why Meenu-amma! Are you getting bored?'

'No, no!'

'City-bred people will naturally find it hard to kill time here.'

'But how do the people of this place spend their time?'

'This village is going to the dogs, because we don't know how to spend our time. Cards, gambling, drink, women. Take this street now... Every house here has a dreadful story to tell!'

'Don't you have a temple here?'

'We have one. But it is not properly looked after. If you'd like to come with me, I can take you to the Panaiyatha temple this evening.'

'Yes. Let's go!'

Meenu was in high spirits that evening. She was on her way to the temple along with Raju and Lakshmi. They left the street behind, and soon found themselves on a path between green fields.

'This village is quite beautiful, Lakshmi', said Meenu.

'The place is all right – it's the people who are bad!'

'But why are you against them?'

'You'd feel the same way if you stayed here long enough!'

They had now reached the temple. A simple and unostentatious place. When she walked round the corridor once, her eyes fell on the Ambassador parked at the entrance. Hariharan was helping a lovely girl out of the back seat. There was a wheel chair parked by the car.

CHAPTER SIX

Meenu had a mild shock when she saw him lift the girl up delicately, as if she were a garland. Then she saw him settle her on the wheel chair beside the car. She felt an instant sympathy for this beautiful and healthy girl who had lost the use of her legs.

He was now holding the chair and speaking to the girl, 'Manju! Look, what a lovely place!'

Manju took in at a glance the small temple amidst the fields, and Meenu under the peepul tree. She gazed at Meenu and then said to him, 'Let's go in.'

He pushed the wheel chair, looking straight ahead, taking care not to let his eyes wander. His expression was serious unlike the bubbly behaviour he had exhibited when she met him before.

'Shall we go now, Meenu?' Lakshmi broke in on her thoughts and added in a whisper, 'It seems that girl cannot walk.'

'Who's she, Lakshmi?'

'I don't know. Maybe his wife.' Meenu wondered if it was possible for a man to be so light-hearted, with a cripple for wife.

'He looks like a film star,' said Lakshmi to whom the cinema spelt glamour.

Meenu laughed.

'What does he want to do here in the village, coming with a sick wife?' wondered Lakshmi.

'Why, Lakshmi, so you've decided that the woman is his wife?'

'It must be his wife.'

'Then maybe they found this place beautiful and wanted to spend a few days here.'

'Not just a few days. They say there are going to settle down and farm here.'

'Who are the 'they' who say so?'

'The people in your Brahmin quarter.' She remembered how the women and children of the whole street had come out and stood staring at the newcomers. By now, the whole village would have managed to ferret out every little detail about him, and yet they did not seem to have asked him who the woman with him was!

She was surprised when he walked past her fixing his gaze on the sky and the temple.

Raju shouted excitedly, 'Look there, Meenu akka!'

Storks were flying over the fields, pure white flocks over the green.

'Aren't they lovely, akka?'

'Oh! How lovely!'

Raju clapped his hand in delight and jumped about wildly. He held her by the waist and danced round her. Meenu looked at him in wonder as if at a stranger. She had never seen his eyes express any emotion except fear and anxiety. Now, watching the storks, his eyes shone with joy.

As if sensing Raju's excitement, the storks flew low and landed on the fields. Raju ran towards them, laughing. At his approach, the birds flew away with a flutter of wings.

'They've all flown away!' cried Raju, disappointed.

'You've got to look at them from afar. They'd be afraid of you if you went nearer.'

'But why should they be afraid of me? I won't hit them!' She was sorry to see his eyes clouding over with fear again. 'All the same, they'd imagine you were after them, to catch them. That's why.'

Lakshmi said, 'It's just like you wanting to escape the moment you see your father.'

'Do be quiet, Lakshmi!'

Raju's face was a picture of gloom. The usual imbecile blankness spread over it. Meenu was sure that her mama had never seen the natural face behind the mask. Nor could he ever understand the ecstasy that the boy had felt at seeing the storks. Laughter, pleasure in innocent, harmless talk – these were not things that led to success or 'prosperity!'

She remembered how Sabhesan had walked over the beautiful kolam pattern that Lalita had drawn. How relentlessly he had dragged his slippered feet over it. She thought of the thrashing he had given Raju. She still heard Raju's cries.

'This house is never going to prosper. Never!'

Why was he so consumed with anger? How could his perpetual anger make anything prosper? What did he hope to achieve with all this strict discipline?

She remembered her mother's frequent assessment of him! 'Well, my brother is hot-tempered, I agree. He never wastes his time or money. What's wrong if he expects the same strict behaviour from others?'

But her mother's opinions were often superficial. If her father had behaved like Sabhesan for a single day, Meenu was sure her mother would have left him. She was not like Lalita, given to enduring everything in silence, with an unfailing smile that seemed to say, 'Nothing serious has happened now...'

'Meenu akka! Look up there! The storks are coming back again!'

And there indeed was a flight of storks, much larger, a dazzling white formation moving against the blue sky.

'Shall we run with them, Raju?'

'Yes! Come on!'

They ran along on the path beside the fields, laughing. Raju followed the flurrying birds with growing excitement. When they finally flew away and vanished in the distance, Raju sat down on a hillock, gasping, his flushed face slit by a grin. Meenu sat down beside him. Here was a Raju she had never seen before.

Suddenly Raju took her hand. 'Please stay with us here, Meenu akka! Please, won't you?'

The longing in those eyes made Meenu feel that this boy deserved all she could do for him. She smiled. 'I can stay here. But then, what about my studies? You know that there's no college here.'

'There is one in town. You can go by bus. It's not too far, Meenu akka!'

Meenu looked thoughtfully at him. How he does ache for love!—Like the parched earth soaking up water!

'Well, let's see,' she said.

Raju hung down his head. 'No, you won't stay on. And I know why, too.'

'And why?'

'You're afraid father would be cross with you as he is with me.'

'Oh no! It's not that.'

'But I know you're afraid of him. But then, Meenu akka, father won't be angry with you!'

The he added rather slowly, 'It's only me that he doesn't like. He doesn't like me at all.' He spoke with adult conviction and a clarity that chilled her to the bone. 'But Raju, it can't be true. You don't find parents not loving their children.'

But Raju shook his head with an air of finality.

'U-hum! My father definitely does not love me! Why else does he beat me whenever he sees me?'

'It's only that mama wants you to study well and grow up and be clever.'

'No, no. He doesn't love me at all!'

'People like him are just hot-tempered. It doesn't mean that such people can't love.'

Raju sat gazing at the sky. She realised that he was in no mood to be convinced.

'Won't we all go up to the sky when we die, Meenu akka?'

She pretended to be amused. 'I have no experience of death, you know!'

'I'm sure we'll go there. Because that's where God is. If only we could have a home in the heavens! It would be just wonderful! Don't you think so, Meenu akka?'

Lakshmi had at last caught up with them. 'O mother mine! So here you are! Whatever did you run like that for? Did you have a race or something?' It was a tired Lakshmi who stood before them.

Meenu laughed, 'Did you go searching for us?'

'Not much of a search. But I was worried.'

'Why ever?'

'Well this is not a safe place for a girl like you. You are quite grown up now. And you're good looking too!'

Meenu burst out laughing.

'What a strange, frightened woman you are, Lakshmi!'

'But one ought to be a little careful at times. You may trust people in the city, but not people in this village. Now, get up both of you! It will soon be dark.'

Meenu stood up, lifting Raju up by the hand. Lakshmi's opinion of the people in the village appeared rather extreme.

Darkness had fallen. Their street was now enveloped in silence with a few oil lamps flickering in their niches on the porches of the houses. Raju's springy walk suggested that he was still lost in thought about a home in the heavens.

Lakshmi whispered to Meenu, 'Look at that house, there!' as they entered the Brahmin quarter of the village.

Meenu turned and looked. She could make out two women sitting on the porch of a house, facing each other. She asked Lakshmi, 'What's the matter there?'

'It's a curious thing, Meenu amma. The woman of that house had been ailing and was laid up for nearly ten years. The husband never bothered to have her treated. His excuse was that he didn't have the means, though he used to drink and spend on himself all the time. The poor woman died only last year. Now the son of the house is going the way of his father. Only, he does everything openly. Those two women you saw there were his wife and his 'second woman'.'

'How can the two of them sit out together like that?'

Lakshmi laughed. 'That's the funny thing about this place. People have lost all sense of shame. The second woman is not even of your caste.'

'There you go again, with your talk of caste.'

'How else can you know about these things?'

'Well, I don't want to know any of these things.'

'Let's leave caste aside them. All I meant was how do people find money for such things, when they complain that they don't have enough even to eat? Does a mistress come for nothing?'

'Why don't you go and ask them?'

'I really would have liked to ask them. But they'll soon be leaving the place. They're selling their land to your mama,' Lakshmi laughed.

Meenu found it hard to understand her mama's voracious appetite for property. What was he doing it for? Whom did he want to please? Or make happy?

And then she stopped in her tracks. There he was, the newcomer with the car, standing at his doorstep. Breaking into a ready grin as she walked past him, he asked: 'Why so long to return from the temple?'

CHAPTER SEVEN

Meenu was surprised. The teasing, light-hearted look was back on his face. But why did he behave at the temple as if he had not seen her at all? Was it because his wife was there with him? If so, she didn't think much of him. She also felt slightly irritated.

'We didn't come by car. We had to walk all the way.' She walked faster, dragging Raju by the hand.

'You're a bold one indeed!' whispered Lakshmi. Meenu quickened her steps to a half-run and reached home. As Meenu and Raju sat down on the porch, Lalita came out with an oil lamp. Setting the lamp in its niche, she said, 'So you're back at last!'

As Meenu looked at Lalita's face, golden in the light of the lamp, she felt a sense of awe. Finding Meenu and Raju with their hands round each other's shoulder and their legs stretched before them on the floor in tired contentment, Lalita laughed.

'You are tired after that trip to the temple, aren't you?'

'Not at all, amma', said Raju, 'can't we go there daily?'

Lalita laughed but said nothing. Meenu surmised that Lalita would not commit herself to anything without Sabhesan mama's permission.

'How did you find the temple, Meenu?'

'A modest temple. But it's so green all the way, it's worth going everyday.'

'The goddess of that temple is a very powerful deity, Meenu. She is taken out in procession, decked out beautifully during festivals. To look at her at those times makes me all a-tremble! But you're laughing.'

'Oh, it's only that,' Meenu started shyly but continued, 'I can't say that I felt any fervour when I looked at the deity in the temple. But now, when I saw you coming, lamp in hand, and looked up at you, well. I felt all a-tremble then!'

Lalita was taken aback. She lowered her eyes after a quick glance at Meenu. 'Don't imagine such things about me, Meenu. I'm a very ordinary woman.'

Meenu had a suspicion that Lalita was more moved than she chose to show.

'But manni! I can't think of you as just an ordinary woman!'

Lalita looked up and laughed.

'Then let me thank you for the compliment, Meenu. You remind me of something that happened in Bombay, where I grew up. In fact, I was in Bombay till I got married. My father worked in a private firm then. The company's flats were in a high-rise building with twenty-six floors and we lived on the first floor. I had always wanted to go and have a look at the top most floors—it looked so extraordinary, something inaccessible from down below. Finally, when father did take me there, I found that except for the choking gusts of wind, those flats at the top were no different from ours down below. No better either. People are much the same, Meenu. None of us is extraordinary.'

'And manni, what about the people on the ground? What did they look like from your perch at the top?'

'Like dolls! Mere dolls!'

Meenu laughed. 'Do you know, manni, when I look at you, I hold my breath and grope for words? It is as if the rest of us were dolls beside you!'

'Where did you learn to speak like that, Meenu?'

'Maybe you are my inspiration!'

'Amma, let Meenu akka stay with us, she can continue her studies here, can't she?'

Lalita looked at Raju thoughtfully for a moment and then she said with some deliberation, 'Yes, Meenu, you could study here. There's a college in town, you know.'

'Is it a good one?'

'Not bad, I think. Tell me, Meenu, why do you want to study further? For the sake of knowledge? Or do you want to work?'

'Both. Who knows what life holds for us in future? It may happen that I'll have to support myself, stand on my feet. Higher education is a 'must' if you want to be independent.'

'You certainly ponder too much for your age, Meenu.' Lalita said looking at her in wonder.

'And you're sure to shape well wherever you study. You needn't worry about which college you go to. Raju wants you to stay here, so why don't you stay?'

'We'll have to think about that.'

'When are your exam results expected?'

'In a couple of days.'

'What's that chattering on the front porch?' Sabhesan's question came roaring from within the house.

All three of them got off the platform in the porch in a panic and went in, not daring to look up.

Sabhesan was shouting at them from the hall. 'With the price of oil what it is, the front lamp is lit as early as five o'clock in this house! And what is one to make of it when the women of the house go and sit on the front platform with a lighted lamp? At this rate, this house is never going to prosper. Never.'

Meenu shut her ears. Lalita went to the kitchen. Raju entered the inner room and soon came out with his schoolbag. Meenu found herself impelled to sit next to him when he sat down with an open book in front of him on the floor.

'You there, how many times have I told you to start doing your lessons as soon as the lamps are lighted? You just want to join the women in their gossip, don't you?'

Meenu noticed that Raju's hands were shaking. He had just started to open his book. She whispered, 'I'm here Raju. Read well.'

Raju began to read, holding her hand. As she felt that clammy, stiff hand in hers, all the exhilaration of the evening left her. Would it be possible for her to stay in this vortex for long, she wondered. How long could she put up with her mama's cantankerous outbursts? He must be getting a sadistic pleasure out of his taunts. Why didn't he realise that it was his own curses that would ruin his house?

Had he ever, at any time, laughed or been gentle with Lalita manni or Raju? She knew from her mother that Lalita studied up to the tenth class at a missionary school in Bombay. She had also heard about their flat in a high-rise building.

And that made her wonder all the more at Lalita. How was it possible for someone with a refined and modern background like that to listen to such non-stop abuse? How could this manni take it all in her stride with a smile? Did she have no self-respect, no dignity? Could it be that she had managed to identify herself with this sort of existence, never thinking ill of anyone, never carping, never nursing a grievance?

Lalita manni was an extraordinary woman—there was not the least doubt about it in Meenu's mind now. What she had censured as a lack of pride and self-respect was perhaps something else—something almost saintly.

'Do we get any dinner today?'

Meenu got up instantly, vexed and indignant. He did not seem to know how to talk civilly. This arrogant man was able to carry on in this fashion only because no one stood up to him here. What if someone dared to talk back? How would he react? Those glowering eyes, those restless hands seemed to hold the threat that any one who dared would soon be dead and buried! This man was mere hulk. All body, no mind!

Meenu set a plate and a glass of water on the floor for her mama and said to Lalita, 'Let mama eat now. Raju and I will eat later.'

Meenu came into the front room. Through the window, she could see a pitch-dark sky. How did people spend their leisure here? One was not even allowed to sit on the platform overlooking the street. There was no radio, no T.V.

'Aiya!'

Meenu heard the call from the front and went to open the street door. She found Sabhesan already at the door, which meant that he had finished his dinner. It was the telegraph-peon at the door. Meenu's heart missed a beat. As Sabhesan opened and read the telegram, his face visibly relaxed. He even began to smile.

'Who is it from?' asked Lalita.

'Meenu has got a first class in her exams, it says here.'

Lalita took Meenu's hands.

'Oh Meenu, I always knew you would, you bright girl.' There was real warmth and happiness in her voice.

'Umm!' Sabhesan grunted his approval.

'I must leave for Madras soon, manni. I'll have to apply for admission to a college.'

With unexpected good humour Sabhesan suggested, 'Why don't you continue your studies here? I'll take you to town.'

Meenu was amazed. How long would his agreeableness least? 'But, is it a good college?'

'Good enough. After all, you are not going to look for a Collector's job. A college is just to keep you occupied till you get married!'

Meenu was aware that it was futile to tell him what she had told her manni. 'I wonder what mother will have to say about it.'

'Who Bala? Why should she have a say in this matter at all?' In a moment, Sabhesan's voice took on an edge. 'Oh well, If you don't like it here, you can leave for Madras. I'm not going to press you to stay.'

The next evening Meenu was on her way to the temple again, holding Raju by the hand. She was still undecided.

'Congratulations!'—It was Hariharan again. With his fine set of teeth flashing a grin and an unspoken assumption that there were no secrets in this village.

'Thanks!' said Meenu.

'The college in town is quite a good one. Satisfaction guaranteed!'

She was confused. What else did he know about her?

'And that's because I'm a Botany lecturer in that college!'

His laughing eyes made her feel uncomfortable.

'Oh! What a surprise! I never thought…'

Raju had started to mutter impatiently. 'Come, let's go now, akka!'

As she started walking again, Raju clung to her. After a while he said with a wistful look at her, 'Please do stay on Meenu akka. Won't you?'

'I think I will, Raju!'—Now she answered him without hesitation, looking at the clear sky far ahead.

CHAPTER EIGHT

'Thoomani maadathu ...'

It was Meenu singing in the front room. The song reached Lalita, busy with her morning routine of drawing kolam. She stopped to listen with eyes and hands off the design for a moment. 'How well she sings!' thought Lalita. It was unbelievable that the blustering Bala could be the mother of a girl like Meenu, beautiful, with a keen mind and the maturity of a twenty-five year old at sixteen. But—and here she smiled—this girl was not docile. She knew her mind and had values of her own. She would never acquiesce in wrongdoing. There was such force and passion in her speech.

An oft-repeated question of Meenu this past month had been, 'What is the secret of your eternal forbearance, manni?'

'This is not really forbearance, Meenu. His anger, fury, abuse—they don't mean a thing really. They're just a veneer. They can be wiped off his soul. If only we could understand that, nothing can possibly affect us. After all, I've been reciting *The Gita* ever since I can remember. Don't you think it's bound to have some effect on me?'

'Do you really mean to say that nothing of this ever disturbs you? That you never feel any hurt? Or anger?'

'Not much really.'

'How I long to grip you hard and shake you out of this numbness! And give you some kind of shock-therapy!'

Lalita stood up, smiling, the bowl of kolam powder in hand. One by one, the women from the neighbouring houses were coming out to sprinkle water on the ground and draw kolams. One in particular was noticeable because of her plastic bucket. She was the newcomer Hariharan's cook. Seeing her sweep stylishly, one was aware that Hariharan had come with a retinue, as well as a car.

The patch of ground in front of teacher Balu's house was still dry. His maid seldom turned up before noon. By the time she began to sprinkle water with a loud splutter, women in the other houses would be preparing to take their siesta, with a wooden door-stop for a pillow, having finished their morning chores.

Krishnan had recovered from his illness and had started playing on the street. Rukmini had sent twice to find out how he was. She had also sent some sweet limes for him. It had been a problem for Lalita to get them to the boy without the knowledge of his father or Sabhesan. What a tangle of problems! Wanting to extricate herself from one problem, had not Rukmini brought upon herself a host of others? Do people make a cult of acquiring difficult problems once they have solved the simpler ones?

The thought suddenly occurred to her that Sabhesan had not yet started shouting this morning!

Sabhesan! A soul steeped in ignorance. A slave to that demon—Ego.

Lalita pulled herself up. What right had she to judge others?

She washed the puja utensils a second time. Let him worship in peace today! One does puja to gain peace of mind. No benefit can accrue from worship done with a raging mind.

Again, she felt an infinite weariness. 'If I hold such debates with myself, it means that my mind is restless; I am not at peace. How stupid of me, then, to boast to Meenu that my mind is untouched by all these going-on!'

Sabhesan finished his bath and came in, daubing bright stripes of sacred ash on his chest.

'We can get Meenu admitted to the college here' he began. 'But she shouldn't start behaving like the students in Madras. She must go to college and come straight back home on time. Girls are not allowed even to step out of the house in this village, once they reach puberty. It is a grave responsibility to have a nubile girl at home.'

Lalita wondered what could have caused this outburst. After all, he himself had suggested that Meenu could continue her studies here. And now he made it appear as if he had given in after much pleading. What could he mean? Oh, never mind. 'That's the way he is.'

'But Meenu is a very sensible girl,' she ventured.

'One can never say how soon a sensible girl will take leave of her senses.'

Lalita hoped Meenu was not listening. She fell silent.

'Why don't you say something?' asked Sabhesan. 'You think I have no right to advise her.'

'You've got every right!' said Lalita appeasingly. 'But I don't think you'll have any cause for worry. I'll keep an eye on her.'

He sat down for his puja without a word. His expression signified that he was not one to be easily appeased.

Lalita woke Raju and sent him to brush his teeth. Her eyes fell on Meenu in the front room, looking out of the window. Disturbed that she might have heard Sabhesan's remarks, she asked, 'Meenu, why did you stop singing? That was a lovely song.'

Meenu turned to her with a half smile: 'Will my staying here add to your problems, manni?'

'Not at all, Meenu. In fact, you'd subtract from them! Stay back, for Raju's sake. You will be a great help to me too.'

Meenu bent her head. 'I don't really know if...'

Lalita broke in. 'I know I'm being rather selfish, Meenu. I thought only of Raju and myself, of how nice it would be for us if you stayed. I didn't give a thought to how uncomfortable you may be here.'

'I don't think I feel uncomfortable here. It's only about the college that I am worried. Is it a good college? With a good library? And then, of course, I'm a bit worried about mama's temper.'

'I've heard that the college has a good library though not many people use it. As for your other worry, don't let it bother you, Meenu.'

'But how can I ignore it?'

'Haven't you seen how drops of water just roll off from the surface of the lotus leaves? We must cultivate that habit of detachment.'

'At my age, sixteen?'

'Already sixteen, aren't you?'

'Sixteen, going on seventeen. Two months more to go, in fact.'

'It's high time then that you practised detachment. For someone as intelligent as you, it shouldn't be difficult.'

'But it seems to need a thick skin, manni.'

'Are you accusing me of having a thick skin?'

'What's all that chatter and laughter early in the morning? The boy has brushed his teeth, but there's no one to give him some milk or coffee.' Sabhesan had made himself heard. Lalita hurried to the kitchen.

Her husband continued, 'Hey boy, you'll have to get your own milk or coffee hereafter. Now that you've finished learning everything else, you can learn a few things like that in future.'

Lalita sighed. She cooled some milk for Raju and called him to the kitchen. Raju came in.

'Who is father shouting at, amma?'

Suddenly Lalita felt like laughing. Often she herself was not sure at whom her husband's barbs were directed.

'Have you given him his milk or coffee?' Sabhesan asked again.

'Yes.'

'Drink it up and go and study in the hall.'

Sabhesan lingered in the kitchen. 'Sankaralinga Iyer's family is going to Madras, do you know anything about it?' he asked.

Lalita stood silent, unable to say 'No'.

Sabhesan went on, 'They're going to sell their land and join their son in Madras.'

'It's going to be rather difficult for him there.'

'Do you imagine he's been very comfortable here? How can anyone expect to be comfortable if all he ever does is to sit idle and eat? Well... what I wanted to tell you was this—I've bought all his lands.'

Lalita listened. That he had chosen to confide in her gave her some satisfaction. But his insatiable greed for land made her squirm. In an attempt to hide her aversion, she busied herself at the oven.

'Did you hear what I said?'

'Yes.'

Sabhesan walked out stiffly, put on his slippers, and staring into the distance, went out stomping as usual over the kolam pattern on the front yard.

Lalita went on with her chores. After a while she found Lakshmi standing in the hall near the kitchen.

'What's it, Lakshmi?'

'Is our Sami in?'

'No. Why? What's the matter?'

Lakshmi lowered her voice and said, 'Sankaralinga Iyer's daughter-in-law is here.'

'Who? Saroja? Ask her to sit down. I'm coming.'

Saroja was standing in the back verandah holding on to a pillar. Her darkly circled eyes and cheeks gave Lalita a sinking feeling. She recalled Sabhesan's words—'I've bought all their lands!'

'Come, Saroja, come in!' cried Lalita.

'It's all right, mami, I'll sit here.'

'It's been long since I saw you. You don't look well.'

Saroja began to cry. 'Saroji amma, please don't cry. After all what can you do if men behave as they do?' said Lakshmi.

Lalita feared that Sabhesan might come back any moment. She gripped Saroja's shoulder.

'Hush! Saroja, don't cry. Tell me, what's the matter?'

Wiping her eyes with the hem of her threadbare sari, Saroja looked up.

'Mami! What can he gain by going to Madras when he has been such a failure here?'

Lalita said nothing.

'Is Madras going to change him, mami?'

'Maybe there's just a chance, Saroja,' she said softly.

'Do you really believe that?' Saroja was now bristling with anger. 'Such golden land we had here. He has ruined it by neglect. There's hardly enough for us to eat. But of course, he must strut about like a Zamindar. The sight of cash rouses all his appetites. And this money from the sale of the land – how long do you expect it to last?'

Lalita hung her head. Was she being accused?

Saroja continued excitedly, 'Do you know, I often feel I should do just what Rukmini did.'

'What sort of talk is that, Saroja?' Lalita tried to sound severe.

'Do you think we women can maintain the prestige of our families when the men show that they care two hoots for their dharma or prestige? They are free to do what they like and have been at it so long that they have become the butt of the village.'

'And, if today we are not able to hold our heads high in our Brahmin quarter, who is to blame for it, mami?'

'Everything is done openly nowadays. The drinking is done at home. Just imagine my plight...'

'I don't have to imagine anything. It is all there, written large on your face and your eyes!'

'When he can behave so atrociously, why can't I leave him? I sometimes think I will...'

Lalita looked closely at her. Where did Saroja think she could go with that face and body of hers? She looked like a corpse.

'Saroja,' Lalita said softly, 'If the men behave foolishly, should we follow suit? What about our children?'

'To hell with them!'

Lalita was taken aback by the vehemence of the outburst. She slipped her hand behind Saroja's shoulders and asked, 'How long is it since you had anything to eat, Saroja?'

Saroja buried her head in her lap, her hunched body shaking with sobs. Lalita got up, beckoning Lakshmi to come in. She went to the store-room, poured out five measures of rice into a small cloth bag and handed it to Lakshmi. 'Take this to Saroja amma,' she said.

Then she called out, 'There you are! Saroja, take the rice home. No need to tell anyone.'

Saroja did not lift her head.

'Saroja, please leave before he comes back,' Lalita pleaded. She was ashamed but she must be careful.

Saroja wiped her eyes and stood up. 'Let me go then, mami.'

Lalita quickly returned to the kitchen. Saroja's plight had moved her. When you are starving, shame and dishonour are insignificant problems. What Saroja had said about her husband and her father-in-law, Sankaralinga Iyer, was quite true. Going to Madras could do them no good.

Suddenly remembering Meenu, Lalita called out to her.

'Yes, manni!'

'Where were you all this while?'

'Oh, just reading something. So, what's the news, manni? Somebody had come to see you, who was it?'

'I'll tell you later. Now you'd better give Raju a bath and get him ready for school.'

CHAPTER NINE

'We have to start at eight-thirty sharp. Have something to eat and get ready to go to college soon.' said Sabhesan in an intimidating voice. He was standing outside Meenu's door.

'Okay, mama.' Her college was due to open today. She had been in a flutter ever since she woke up that morning. What sort of boys and girls was she going to meet? Would they turn out to be sprightly and cheerful as her chattering companions in Madras? But the more she observed people in the street, the more convinced she was that they had forgotten how to be happy. And that was why Hariharan's ready grin seemed so out-of-place – even exaggerated and unnatural. The local population was rather stodgy.

No girl past puberty could step out of her house in this village. Meenu was surprised at this. But she also grieved for the girls. What could they find to do inside those dark rooms the whole day? How long could they go on embroidering or crocheting dancing peacocks and 'WELCOME'? And how long could they gossip about their womenfolk and goings-on? How did the patch of sky seen through their windows affect them? For this was all they saw of the world outside. Did their dreams ever end like fairytales? Living among such hard-headed realists, those girls were sure to be fed up with the old village stories. As a new character appearing on an old scene, Meenu must seem quite interesting to them! And what about Sabhesan? If, for some reason, she became the subject of loose talk here, how would he take it?

'Meenu, haven't you combed your hair yet?'

'Yes, manni. I'm coming!' She wore a fresh sari, powdered her face lightly and put a dot of kumkum on her forehead. She hurried to the kitchen and sat down to breakfast.

She had not quite finished eating when Sabhesan's voice reached her. 'What? Not ready yet?'

Meenu looked at her watch. It was only eight twenty. Ten minutes more. But she got up. 'I'm ready mama!'

'What about your curdrice?' whispered Lalita.

'I'll have it after I come back.'

She saw Sabhesan's hooded bullock cart in the street. So she was to go to college by bullock cart! Slightly bewildered, she climbed into the cart.

'You can go up to the bus stop by cart. From there, you have to take the bus that goes up to the gates of the college.' Sabhesan spoke as if he were addressing a party of tourists. Meenu smiled.

The tinkling of the bullock's bells and the spreading view of the green fields made it hard for her to believe that she was really going to college.

And the college itself was more like a government office than an educational institution. It was gloomy, with no sound of talk or laughter. Girls in chintz long skirts and half-saris, their hair coiled and tightly plaited, stood in small clusters. Meenu saw Hariharan's Ambassador parked in the shade of a tree and thought, 'Lucky that I'll be studying History. I needn't have anything to do with the Botany lecturer...'

The lecturers taught much better than she had expected. She took a few books out of the library. When she returned home in the evening she felt exhausted, as if she had returned from a long journey. Lalita was waiting for her at the threshold.

'How was it, Meenu?' she asked.

'Not bad at all.'

'Good!' Lalita laughed.

Once she had her tiffin and coffee, she felt ready to go to the temple. She wanted to laugh and run hand-in-hand with Raju looking at the birds in the sky.

'Shall we go to the temple, Raju?'

Before she could finish, Raju came skipping up to her, abandoning the top he was playing with. Lakshmi was to accompany them. 'Why, manni, won't you come with us?' asked Meenu.

'No, Meenu. Your mama will be back soon. He won't like me to lock up the house and go out.'

'Is there anything that he does like?'

Lalita shook her head. 'There you go again!'

Meenu took Raju's hand and left the place, laughing.

In front of the third house was the Ambassador, somewhat dusty now. As she walked past the house, she had a feeling that she was being watched; but she did not turn to look. In front of Balu the teacher's house, Krishnan was playing marbles all by himself.

'Coming to the temple with us, Krishnan?'

'No. There's no one to mind the house. Father has gone shopping.'

Meenu felt sorry for him. The children in this street were prematurely old. They bore the weight of their parents' sins. They were likely to forget how to laugh before they grew up. But soon they met young Gopali, farmer Govindasami's son, who was in high spirits. Grinning haughtily, he accosted Raju with, 'Where're you going, you loafer?' Meenu was surprised by the arrogance of his tone. Raju answered innocently, 'To the temple.'

Those two women on Sankaralinga Iyer's verandah were there as before, seated facing each other. The backyard was visible from the front door and the house seemed empty.

Once they had left the brahmin street behind, Meenu asked Lakshmi, 'Who came to our house this morning Lakshmi?'

'Sankaralinga Iyer's daughter-in-law. She cried the whole time.'

'What for?'

'What a question! For a hundred reasons. What with a reckless husband and moving to a strange place... But her worst problem is hunger. Our amma knows it. She gave her some rice today. But how long can amma help her without Sami's knowledge?'

They were among the green fields now. Such greenery and such hunger!

Lakshmi continued indignantly, 'These are fertile lands with plenty of golden 'ponni' rice. But land doesn't yield its riches without hard work. If you spend the whole day drinking, gambling and chasing women, what does the earth care about you?'

Meenu nodded. These poor people in the Brahmin quarters were themselves to blame for their misery. That's why a farmer's boy like Gopali dares to call Raju a 'loafer'.

'Look! Meenu akka, look there! The storks again!'

She turned and saw a group of seven to eight storks dazzlingly white, sitting close together, as if posing for a photograph. Meenu took Raju's hand in hers and together they ran gaily towards the birds.

She heard Lakshmi laughing behind her. 'What a heap of trouble this girl is!' The narrow path among the fields was wet. Meenu lifted up her sari slightly and let Raju run in front. The storks rose with a sudden swish. Raju's face lighted up. His cheeks glowed. His eyes shone with a rare glint that intrigued Meenu.

'Come on!' She said, 'Let's go to the temple first. We can look at the storks when we return.'

'Shall we run now?'

'Here we go!' She ran as if she were Raju's age. They ran till they reached the outer corridor of the temple, where Meenu chased Raju. She came to a sudden jolt – she had bumped into someone. When she recovered her balance, she found that she was being held by the shoulders. She looked up in confusion and found herself face to face with Hariharan.

He stood before her, intent and smiling. Meenu slid out of his grip and muttered a shy apology.

He laughed. 'Training for some track event, are you? Rest for a bit now. I too feel like letting myself go when I look at these open fields. But I can't give way to my impulses – too old for that!'

'But I'm not!' laughed Meenu.

He looked at her and she did not miss the point of his scrutiny. She laughed. 'One is as old as one feels,' she explained.

'Thank God! I've heard the ten-year-olds of this village talk like forty-year olds. You're a welcome change. How was college today?'

'Better than I expected.'

'How did you get there?'

'By bullock-cart for part of the way and then by bus.'

'Why go to so much trouble? I drive to college. You can come with me.'

Meenu looked at him in surprise. 'That'll be the end of me here! My mama will pack me off to Madras by the next train. He has laid down several conditions if I am to stay on here.'

'I wonder he didn't think of a ban on running through the open fields!'

'I must remember that in future.'

Raju, short of breath, came running up to them. 'Come, akka. Let's go round the shrine.'

Hariharan went with them.

She noticed that his car was not parked outside. Obviously, he had not brought the girl today. No one seemed to know who the girl was.

He suddenly asked, 'Where's that maid who came with you?'

'How do you know she came with us?'

He looked self-conscious. 'I saw the three of you start from home.'

Did it mean that he came here because he had seen her coming? But Meenu at once dismissed the thought.

'Oh, Lakshmi must be on her way. Raju and I came running,' said Meenu and added with some hesitation, 'You brought someone along to the temple the other day…'

He glanced at her for a brief moment and said gazing at the sky, 'That was my sister.'

'Poor girl!' said Meenu involuntarily. 'How long has she been like that – unable to walk?'

'Fifteen years now. She had polio when she was just two. No treatment seemed to work for her. I came here mainly for her sake. She is fed up with Madras. Luckily, I got a job here. Father owns a lot of land, but I'm not interested in farming.'

'And your father and mother?'

'They are here, with me,' he replied, 'but they don't come out much. You see, looking after my sister is quite a job.'

That made her glance up at him. He gazed at the sky again, with a sad smile.

'Her illness has warped her mind. She is in an ugly mood half the time.'

Meenu recalled the intent look on the girl's face as she sat gripping her wheel chair, determined not to look around.

'She's a pretty girl.'

'But she doesn't like my talking to any pretty girl.'

'Why?' she asked in some surprise.

He was about to reply when he saw Lakshmi coming towards them, which meant he should not continue the conversation.

CHAPTER TEN

The priest waved the burning camphor before the idol of the Goddess Panaiyatha. Lakshmi and Raju patted their cheeks in pious submission. In between, Hariharan glanced up at Meenu and smiled. Much sad experience lies behind that ready smile, thought Meenu. Lakshmi's sudden appearance had cut their conversation short – a disappointment. She had begun to wonder why he had felt free to discuss his domestic problems with her – a stranger. When the priest brought the camphor plate to her, she held her hands over the flame, then pressed her palms to her eyes. 'Let's go back now!' she said to Raju.

She nodded a brief goodbye to Hariharan and started walking homeward, thinking of him all the way. Every house in their street seemed to harbour a problem. These newcomers had brought theirs, in addition. If as Hariharan says, his sister has been affected mentally, does it mean that she's off her mind? Or just hysterical?

'What's wrong with that girl? Did you find out?' asked Lakshmi, echoing Meenu's thoughts.

'She lost the use of her legs when quite young.'

'Is that so? Now, what's the use of all their wealth to her? She's his wife, isn't she?'

'No, his sister.'

On their way back there were no storks. It was as if the birds honoured her new sadness. Raju came at a half-run, chasing butterflies and plucking wild flowers.

'Why do you live alone, Lakshmi? Have you no one of your own?'

'Huh. I've been married. I've had my fill of that. No more for me, thank you.'

'You speak as if you were a hundred years old!'

'I've been through that much! How can a woman live with a husband who ill-treats her? Why should she? I told him to go to hell!'

'And quite right too, Lakshmi!' Meenu applauded, laughing.

'It's all right for me to do so because my people don't mind. It's not quite the same for people of your caste. Didn't you see what happened to that Rukmini? You may think it's all because she's living with another man. But even if it were not so, a woman who leaves her husband is viciously slandered – a hundred poisoned tongues would wag.'

'Far better to be insulted by society than be ill-treated by a husband.'

'But what does a woman gain by all that defiance, if she can't earn a living? As for me, I can always wash utensils in a few houses for a living. Can upper-caste women do that? The educated ones can try to get a job. But what of the rest? Only those who have gone without food know what it's like. That's why Rukmini chose to go to that man in town. And now Saroja would like to do the same. But what man would take her in, with that corpse-like body of hers?'

Meenu shuddered. 'That's an ugly thing to say, Lakshmi.'

'Truth is always ugly, Meenu amma.'

They had reached the Brahmin quarter. In the fading light, the street's unlit houses looked ghostly. Upon seeing them, a passer-by commented: 'What's this place coming to! Grown-up girls have started coming out on the streets!'

Lakshmi pulled Meenu on. 'Walk on,' she said, 'But don't reply.'

'Who is that?'

'Some busybody with nothing to do. If you bother with talk of that sort, you'll never finish your studies.'

A lamp was lit at their porch. Meenu remembered how Sabhesan had carped about lighting it early. He had an evil tongue.

Lalita was in the hall. She had a harassed look.

'Don't go to the temple so late in the evening, Meenu. I just don't know how to pacify your mama.'

'Has he returned, then?'

'Yes, but he's gone out again. He didn't like your going to the temple.'

Exasperated, Meenu said: 'Well, I'm not going to be cowed by him like you. I'll answer him back. I'm going to take him on.'

'Aiyaiyo!' cried Raju, terrified. 'He'll hit you if you do that! He hits me when I don't answer him. But, he'll hit you if you dare to answer.'

Meenu laughed. 'Did you hear that, manni? What things he knows! And you say he's simple! Come on, Raju! Let's be good now and do our homework.'

Meenu showed Raju how to do his sums and then settled down to read. She wondered how she could spend the whole day, cooped up in this house. She would suffocate if she did not go out into the open in the evenings. How long could she look at the portia tree? Or contemplate the walls of the hall? 'I can't do that mama,' she imagined herself saying. 'No. I'll get claustrophobic. I can't be like manni. I can't recite *The Gita* and live like a drop of water on a lotus leaf.'

'Have those gadabouts returned yet?' Sabhesan's voice from the hall made her want to giggle. But Raju, she found, had given a start and dropped his pencil. She heard Lalita's low voice, 'Yes, they're back.'

'Tongues have started wagging already, do you know?'

Meenu sprang up ready for battle and walked up to Sabhesan. Looking steadily at him, she said, 'I went to the temple with Lakshmi; and I'm back home directly from the temple. If people here must wag their tongues, let them. We don't have to mind them. It's much better for Raju to go for a walk with me than to play with those boys.'

Sabhesan turned livid. 'You don't have to walk till dark.'

'In future, I promise to be back before it gets dark. Is that okay?' she asked smiling.

Sabhesan was still vexed. But he said, 'Okay, Okay. Get on with your studies. No more chatting, both of you!'

'He didn't beat me, see?' said Meenu, laughing softly. Raju glanced down and continued with his writing.

This bully thrives on lack of opposition, thought Meenu. What if Manni and Raju stood up to him! His eyes can't brook it. He needs them as victims. The ties of family, wife and son mattered little to him, the absolute sadist that he was.

Amazing that all these years with him had not embittered Lalita manni. She even had genuine affection for him. It was not easy to understand her. Does *The Gita* have this power to ennoble people? Her mother Bala was also in the habit of reciting *The Gita* as she went about her chores in the kitchen. She was still her old irascible self in spite of all that. Lalita manni seemed to be a serious practitioner of *The Gita*'s teachings. Maybe she was born a yogi!

Sabhesan's voice reached her from beyond the hall.

'Who gave you permission to give her that rice? Tell me.'

That voice brought Meenu down with a thud from the hoary heights of History and the East India Company. There was no reply from Lalita.

'I am asking you a question, answer me.'

Lalita said softly, 'I just couldn't stand the sight of Saroji standing there crying, hungry yet unwilling to ask for rice.'

'So it never occurred to you to get my permission!'

'You were not home.'

'You didn't tell me after I came home, either.'

'I had meant to. But forgot.'

'Lies! You have quite a few secrets from me, I know. If you had the least respect for me, you won't behave this way.'

'Please forgive me. It was such a small matter that it slipped my memory.'

'Small matter? Does it seem 'small' to you? As if you were descended from some Maharaja! I am the one who toils in this house. It is my labour that brought that grain home. You give it away without asking me and then you dare to conceal it from me.'

Meenu listened with growing agitation. What a mean mind he had! What if she went and confronted Sabhesan now? Doesn't a wife have any rights in her own home?

Then she heard Lalita's voice, 'I won't do any thing without asking you hereafter.'

Meenu felt cheated. What a tame ending! Why does Lalita manni apologise for a good and humane act? This was no way to handle mama Sabhesan. A thought struck her: What if he was fed up with all this submission and was craving for a good fight? When she stood up to him the other day, he had retreated. She must teach Lalita the technique of tackling him.

'That's mere eyewash. You are good at playacting. That's what you are.'

Meenu heard the loud bang of something being flung against the wall. It was followed by Sabhesan's heavy footsteps across the hall. Then came the sound of the front door being opened and his stepping out. Meenu went to the kitchen.

Sabhesan's plate had rolled on to a corner and Lalita was sitting on the floor in a dazed state.

'What happened, manni?'

Lalita looked up at her without betraying any emotion and said, 'Oh, nothing. Come on, the two of you, have your dinner.' Then she picked up Sabhesan's plate and took it to be washed.

She smiled at Meenu as she said, 'These are everyday happenings, Meenu. You are not supposed to pay any attention to all these things.'

'Not pay attention? That's something I can't do, ever!'

'Meenu, please! Now go and bring Raju along.'

Lalita served them in silence.

'Won't you join us, manni?'

'Not yet. I'll have something later.'

Not likely, thought Meenu. She finished her meal in silence and began to do her lessons. She found it impossible to concentrate. Sabhesan's angry voice kept reverberating in her mind.

Hearing something, Meenu pricked up her ears. Someone seemed to be singing from somewhere at the back of the house. She could make out the words of the prelude to *The Gita*:

Parthaya prati bodhitam...

Thus spake the Lord to Arjuna ...

Meenu walked towards the melodious voice that chanted the verses:

Brahman yaadhaaya ....

Padma patram ivaam bhasa.

Unmoistened, untouched by water,

Lotus leaves float on the pond.

Unsullied, unattached, likewise,

The yogi performs his duties.

As she reached the open courtyard at the back, she found Lalita sitting on the floor, face upturned, looking at the sky.

Suddenly, Lalita buried her face between her knees and began to sob.

CHAPTER ELEVEN

The tears flowed freely. All the pent up anguish of the past years had rushed headlong and forced the floodgates open.

After a while, her sobs subsided, giving way to melancholy despair. She had been defeated. Bitterly, hopelessly defeated.

Lalita looked up at the stars again. Did they hold a message of hope for her? As she looked deep into the depths of the blue-black sky, the whole universe seemed to come to a sudden standstill, as if it was in silent sympathy with her grief. She felt a chill pass through her, as she heard a voice – very near and very clear. It was her dead father's voice intoning his favourite hymn,

'Thunjum podu azhaimin...

When in the throes of pain and sorrow,

Call upon Him, chant His name!

Lalita felt her father's presence there, in front of her. Her heart gave a leap. He must have descended from among the stars of the sky to share her burden of sorrow. To wipe her tears away.

Yes this was her father. Her father, who had been blessed with the gift of compassion. A man who had lived like a rishi, a sage, for whom wealth and fame had meant little.

Meenu placed a hand softly on Lalita's back. Lalita snapped out of her trance. The sight of Meenu standing there, looking at her with eyes softened by sympathy, revived Lalita's earlier misgivings. How this young girl would be affected by all the unpleasant things happening in this house, she wondered.

Meenu asked in a barely audible whisper: 'Why, manni?'

'Why what?' countered Lalita, with a smile.

'Why are you crying?'

'You often wonder if I am a woman of flesh and blood. Don't you? Here's proof that I am a woman, after all.'

Meenu avoided looking at her and glanced up at the sky as she said, 'Don't give way to grief, manni. It's just that Sabhesan mama thinks he's proving his manhood by hurting you. He's a chauvinist, a terrible male chauvinist.'

Finding Lalita silent, she continued, 'The twentieth century is about to end. But the way you behave, it is as if you were living in some mythological era. You are bent on acting out the role of a 'pativrata', the chaste and ever-obedient wife. It just will not do to let these males go scot-free. If we keep appeasing every whim of theirs, keep bending our backs for them to whip, every male will become a Sabhesan.'

Lalita took Meenu's hands and made her sit beside her.

'You remind me of those descriptions of warriors in our classics. It seems those soldiers had a problem during times of peace since their shoulders and arms would begin to itch for battle. You seem to have an itch for battle, too. But there is something called Peace, isn't there?'

'What is peace? Is it a dumb, docile acceptance of humiliation? Didn't you break down now and cry because even you couldn't endure it any further?'

'Do you think I cried because I felt humiliated?'

'If you deny it, you are a big, bad hypocrite.'

'Well, call me names, if you like. You are not likely to understand whatever I might say.'

'Is it Vedanta, by any chance?'

'Call it what you will, but it's something I believe in.'

'I promise to make an effort to understand. Now tell me, why did you cry?'

Lalita hesitated as if she had been asked to share her innermost secrets. This impatient, defiant girl was in no mood to be convinced. But she was prepared to try.

'Meenu, my father used to say, there is but one thing we have to cry for, and that is man's ignorance.'

'What may that mean?'

'As I have been telling you, man goes astray because of his ignorance. He goes after the transient and loses sight of the enduring, permanent values.'

Meenu laughed. 'That's funny. So when mama abused you, you wept for all of humanity and its ignorance!'

'Think what you will. But I did feel sorry for him. The way he refuses to go beyond the little circle he has imprisoned himself in... He must be woken up.'

Meenu laughed louder. 'But how does your crying help? Some people have to be cudgelled and kicked to get them awake. That's the way to deal with Sabhesan mama. He won't understand any of your philosophy ever. Not in this birth.'

'Why don't you have some faith in people, Meenu?'

'Not in Sabhesan mama. No way. Sorry. I think you are in a way responsible for his behaviour. If only you stood up to him, he'd not have grown into such a monster. You have boosted his ego with your dumb, submissive ways.'

Meenu had spoken her mind.

It was her prerogative as Sabhesan's niece. But Lalita had difficulty accepting her analysis.

'We have no right to censure our elders, Meenu,' she said, limply.

Meenu looked at her in exasperation. 'Our rights as women are at stake here. I am all the more angry because this male happens to be my mama.'

'Shhh, Meenu. I don't think of people as male or female when I feel sorry for them. My heart goes out to anyone who acts foolishly.'

'You mean to say, you see no difference between a poor abused woman like Rukmini and a sexist tyrant like a Sankaralinga Iyer or a Sabhesan!'

'Yes, Meenu,' said Lalita with a sad smile.

'If that's what you think, you manni, you are the greatest fool of them all!'

Lalita laughed in spite of herself.

Then came a shout from behind. 'So here you are! Enjoying the moonlight chattering and laughing! The front door left unbolted all the while.'

Lalita stood up instantly. So, Sabhesan had come in without making the slightest noise.

'And you, don't you have college tomorrow?'

'Yes, mama.'

'If you gossip the whole time, how can you ever study anything?'

Seeing Meenu leave without a word in protest, Lalita relaxed. She went in and gulped tumbler after tumbler of water to silence the rumblings of her empty stomach.

Sabhesan had gone to the well to wash his face and feet. Raju had rolled away from the mat on which he had been sleeping. Lalita pulled him back and lay down to sleep.

A weariness overtook her.

'You are the greatest fool of them all!'

Was there some truth in that conclusion of Meenu's?

Lalita felt that she had never left the starting point despite her long journey of fifteen years. What had she to show for all those years of marriage? Fifteen years, spent like the bullock going round and round the central pillar in the village oil-press.

She had entered this house as a bride of fifteen. These years ought to have been years of growth, development, maturity, achievement. But no, nothing like that had happened.

At fifteen, her heart had been free of rancour. She had never been inclined to take anyone amiss. Having grown up with her father's example before her, she could not have been otherwise.

For some reason, her father had developed a sudden aversion to Bombay, disillusioned with the glamour of city life. He had felt the call of Mother Nature. He used to tell Lalita, I must get you married into a rural family, to some young man who lives off the land. I want you to enjoy the charms of country life. People who live amidst the greenery of nature are sure to have a heart that can still feel some love and compassion. City people are just empty shells without souls.

Lalita was lying awake in the darkened room alongside Raju on the floor. A wry smile played at her lips, as she thought: Her father was well versed in Vedanta, but had no inkling of reality or the shape of things to come. He had not seen people who lived amidst the beauties and bounties of nature, but were untouched by it. People with deadened souls. If he had had the least idea of what life was like here, he would not have married her off to Sabhesan on the strength of somebody's recommendation.

But Father was, by then, a man in a hurry. He lived for just a fortnight after her wedding.

CHAPTER TWELVE

Lalita felt the salt of her tears on her lips. She could still see her Kittu mama from Calcutta as he put up a fight with her father in those weeks before her wedding.

'Where's the need for all this unholy hurry to marry Lalita off?' her mama had asked. 'She's only fifteen and still in school. What makes you push a city-bred, English-educated girl like her into a marriage with some glum faced country bumpkin?'

Her father was silent for a few seconds. Then he smiled at his brother. His countenance glowed with a quiet pride as he began to speak softly, 'I have trained Lalita to lead a content life with no great expectations in whatever situation she might find herself in. Don't judge her by her age or 'convent' education. If I say anything more you will think I am boasting.'

'Quite the contrary. It's because I know what a treasure she is, that I don't want you to marry her off in a hurry. As for this young man, Sabhesan, we seem to know very little about him or his background.'

'Lalita will understand why I chose a country life for her. Sabhesan is a B.A. He has enough lands and property. He seems to be a young man of good habits and sound values. Absolutely nothing ostentatious about him. What more can we hope to find out about anyone?'

As Kittu mama sat grim and un-convinced, Lalita's father continued, 'I have full faith in my daughter. She can be happy anywhere. She's a stranger to envy or anger or dejection. She has nothing but love for everyone.'

'But will that fellow Sabhesan understand all this?'

'It's his loss, if he doesn't.'

The memory of that proud statement made Lalita uncomfortable.

I am just an ordinary woman, she told herself. Father's praise was intoxicating. But it was exaggerated. Let me just remember the core of his teaching: 'Let your love be without expectations.' Yes. Love can be the one constant in life. Unsullied love, unaffected by anything that might happen.

Lalita felt a hand upon her. The violence of the grip brought her hurtling down to the present. As she turned, she could feel Sabhesan's hot breath upon her. She sensed the vulnerability latent in that violence. He seemed to be torturing himself all the time. She caressed his face as if he was a defeated child coming running to his mother to be consoled.

How dark his world seemed to be! What did he hanker after? Wealth? He had enough of it. And here was a wife ready with her love. What was all this frenzy and fury for? Why this refusal to be happy. Why this resentment at seeing anyone else happy? Why this self-inflicted torture, why?

Sabhesan's embrace was demanding, overpowering. If this makes you happy, let it be so. I don't mind.

She stroked the hand that held her tight. How could he forget all the warmth and closeness of his nights, the moment he opened his eyes in the morning? How tightly he shut himself up within himself! He never uttered a single word when he came to her at night, she remembered. Was it that he was afraid he might say a kind word or two in a weak moment? Miserly with his love as with his money. Both equally futile, but pleasing to the egotist in him. Meenu's words came back to her, 'He's a chauvinist, a terrible male chauvinist!'

But Meenu, what can be done about it now? Chauvinism, phobia, mania, whatever way you call it, ideas and attitudes handed down from time immemorial cannot be changed by your taking out processions and waving banners.

Lalita sighed. If only all this darkness can be driven out and a new era be born naturally, just as a new day is born following the night! If only...

That it was not going to be a natural birth was brought home to her quite forcefully and quite soon – in fact, as soon as the next day dawned.

Lalita had just finished drawing the morning kolam and was making coffee when she heard Sabhesan shouting from the backyard. Here we go again, thought Lalita. But why so early? She hastened to the rear of the house.

Face flushed, and eyes fiery, Sabhesan glared at her. It was difficult to believe it was this man who had held her in a yearning embrace at night.

'Where's the water-pot and the rope for drawing water from the well?' he shouted.

Had she forgotten to take them inside from the open yard before locking up for the night yesterday? What if it had been stolen? Lalita hurried to the well saying, 'But it was here …'

'Am I blind that I can't see it here? Did you remember to take it in last night?'

'Sorry, I forgot.'

'How could you forget a thing like that?'

She hung her head in silence.

He must have forgotten all about his tantrums the previous night. Anyway, he was not sensitive enough to gauge the depth of her hurt and shock, when he had asked her, 'Who gave you permission to give her that rice?' No woman can go about her routine chores as if nothing had happened, after her husband had kicked off his plate midway through dinner and left in a rage. She couldn't muster the indifference of a robot. She didn't expect Sabhesan to understand any of that.

Sabhesan made a threatening move, 'I am asking you a question. And you stand there with not a single word in answer.'

She looked down mumbling, 'I just don't know how I could forget to bring that pot in.'

Gritting his teeth, he sprang at her and slapped her hard. 'If the woman of the house keeps chatting and laughing till midnight in the moonlit yard, how can she remember such things? At this rate, this house is never going to prosper. Never!'

As usual, he was working himself up into a rage. Still, she ought to have been more careful, thought Lalita.

'I've been careless. Please forgive me.' She said.

'You can commit a murder and then say 'It was a mistake. Forgive me!' Thieves thrive on the carelessness of people like you.'

'I've got another rope somewhere. Shall I bring it?'

'You don't have to fetch and carry for me. You'll have so many important things to attend to.'

It was only then that she noticed the spare rope on the ground. Obviously, he had already taken it out. She went to the kitchen and brought a brass pot for drawing water.

'How many spares have we left?'

'None.'

'Bear that in mind!'

Sabhesan was still muttering. 'What do you care if something is stolen? You seem to have descended from some Maharaja...'

Lalita returned to the kitchen. It was sad that burglaries were on the rise.

'What happened, manni?' Meenu called out loudly. 'Mama's morning greetings are much louder than usual!'

'There's been a little theft last night, Meenu.'

'What?'

'I left the drawing-rope and pot out at the well last night. Forgot to bring them in before locking up the back door.'

'What a joke!' cried Meenu, 'I brought the things in last night and kept them in the store-room.'

'Go and tell your mama that!' said Lalita visibly relieved.

Soon Sabhesan's loud voice rang out again.

'Who asked you to do it? If you start doing these things, those who ought to do them will become lax. As it is, she's so forgetful about everything.'

Lalita went almost happily about her work pretending not to have heard any of this. She took Sabhesan's coffee to him on the swing in the hall. She would have liked to start a conversation, but the lingering anger on her husband's face was forbidding. So she returned to the kitchen.

Sabhesan drank the coffee and plonked the empty tumbler down.

'I'm going out. Let everyone do her own work!'

Meenu made sure that her mama had left the place before she looked at Lalita. They laughed together for long. Meenu was the first to speak. 'Remember how the saying goes, manni? 'A person can fall down, and still claim his moustache didn't gather any dust.' Doesn't mama ever admit to dust on his moustache, manni? Does he ever own up a mistake?'

'But then Meenu, he hasn't got a moustache, at all.'

Unexpectedly Raju interrupted, 'Who's it, Meenu akka? The man without a moustache?'

'Just you and me, Raju!' Meenu laughed.

'It's getting late for college, Meenu!' reminded Lalita.

'I'll be ready in a jiffy!'

It was only after Meenu and Raju had their breakfast and left that Lalita remembered Sabhesan had not yet returned.

Lakshmi was away at the market. Lalita came to the porch and looked out.

The street looked deserted. But there was quite a crowd in front of the last house – Sankaralinga Iyer's. She wondered why. There was still a week for them to leave for Madras.

She saw Lakshmi hurrying towards her. She seemed panicky. There were tears on her face.

'What is it, Lakshmi?'

'Saroji – that Sankaralinga Iyer's daughter-in-law, has hanged herself!'

'What?' Her heart missed a beat. She could feel tears welling up in her eyes.

CHAPTER THIRTEEN

'Now, Lakshmi, do tell me properly,' said Lalita, straining to see more clearly.

Lakshmi sat down on the platform and tried to be calm. 'What's there to say, amma? She has hanged herself from a rafter in the back verandah. It must have happened some time early this morning before sunrise. Nobody seems to have noticed it till about eight o'clock. They thought she'd gone for her bath to the river. Think of one's own people at home behaving like that! Thoo!' She spat. 'Animals are kinder than men.'

Anger and sorrow were writ large on Lakshmi's face. Her lips quivered, she shook her head from side to side. Lalita stood staring at her with unblinking eyes.

'The children must have thought of their mother as soon as they began to feel hungry. But even when the younger son cried for her, the father seems to have shouted him down: 'That woman is sure to be gossiping with someone. Wait till she comes back and I'll break her legs!' Well, it was the younger boy who discovered his mother first.'

Lalita went cold with horror. What must it have been like for the little boy?

'Let the children go to hell!' Lalita remembered Saroji's words. Intense hatred must have driven her to death.

'Lakshmi,' she said, 'Look after the house for a while. And if Sami happens to come home tell him.'

'But I saw Sami there!'

'Let me go there, then.'

'Yes. I'll stay right here. You can go, amma.'

Lalita left. Her tongue felt dry. There was a throng of men in front of the house. She made her way to the back street and entered the house through the back door.

All the women of the street were there, seated on the back verandah that circled the open courtyard. The sight of the 'second woman' of Saroji's husband among them was disconcerting. These people were not too seriously affected even by death or suicide. The body, covered with a sheet, lay on the floor in the hall, no one beside it. Men had gathered in the front, while women sat in the backyard. Saroji's children stood in a corner unable as yet to grasp the full seriousness of the situation, no yet aware of the full depths of their own sorrow.

Ganesan Padaiyachi's wife, Neelu, spoke to Lalita first.

'Look at what this Saroji has done, amma. What a terrible thing to do!'

Lalita said nothing.

Somebody embroidered on Neelu's remark. 'Who can tell what perversions the mind can think of, once the heart is burdened with suffering?'

'And it was no ordinary suffering. What a lot she had to bear! What a tangle of problems! Isn't there some limit to what a woman can bear? See that rafter there? That's where she was found hanging.'

Lalita sat down heavily. She took no part in the conversation. Her bit of the verandah was dark and provided some privacy. Fodder used to be stacked there, but now the place was used for stacking firewood and dried cowpat.

Lalita could see Saroji as she had stood before her not long ago, holding on to the pillar, her shoulders shaking with sobs... 'Do you really believe he'll change?'

Saroji had borne so much for so long! What was it that gave her the final push? The prospect of moving to the city? The thought of the shame, and humiliation that would be her lot there, as it had been here?

'There is nobody like you in Madras for me to turn to, mami.'

As Lalita recalled her words, pity welled up in her. A body wasted by hunger. A mind worn by suffering. O Saroja! How many women are there like you? All too many!

'No. You can't understand. Only those who have gone through what I've suffered can understand me. My sufferings were real. This was the only way I knew how to end them.'

But Saroji could not do what Rukmini had done. Not knowing where to go, she was now lying there alone in the hall, dead.

Rukmini's way had been a kind of death too – death of the soul.

'It seems the police must be informed before the body can be removed. That means it will be past noon before anything can be done.'

Lalita went to the two boys – Saroji's children – who stood stricken. She put her hands on their shoulders.

'You must be hungry,' she said.

'Yes.' Replied the younger boy.

'Then come along with me and have something to eat.' The boys jumped up at once.

As she went out with the children, she could hear someone say: 'I was just wondering if it would be all right to give them food with the body still lying there.'

Really! Lalita's heart went out to the children with their tousled hair, their dried skin, their shorts hanging about them in tatters.

But why? For what fault of theirs, Saroji?

'Let them go to hell!' Lalita was still troubled by those words.

Lakshmi was still there on the porch when she got home.

'The children are very hungry, Lakshmi. Bring the banana leaves for them to eat from. Let me have a bath first. I'll come and serve them.'

Lakshmi rose. 'All right. But you know you'll have to answer for it when Sami comes back!'

Lalita did not stop to answer her. When she entered the kitchen, she thought of Sabhesan kicking his plate off halfway through the meal last night.

Quickly she made some mixed-rice and brought it to the boys who were seated on the floor, their arms pressed tightly round their empty stomachs. They looked up, their faces bright with expectation as she entered. She watched them devour what she had served. The thought kept recurring: 'How could you find it in your heart to do such a thing?'

The boys finished eating and picked up the plantain leaves and went to the back of the house to throw them away. Then they washed their hands and prepared to leave. 'We're going back, Mami.'

'All right. Come here whenever you feel hungry.'

'But we'll be leaving for Madras.'

'Till you leave, then.'

'Okay.'

Lalita watched them leave. They had not said a word about their mother. Nothing at all about how she had hung from the rafter and was now lying flat on the floor of the hall. They had just felt relief in solving their immediate problem. Young realists.

Remembering that she must send lunch to Sankaralinga Iyer's family, she got Lakshmi to pluck some raw bananas from the trees at the back.

'Who knows how long it will be before the body can be removed?' said Lakshmi, 'The street will have to go hungry till then.'

'You weep for Saroji. Can't we fast for her, Lakshmi?'

'True.'

Lakshmi went away, but was soon back, 'Amma, they've removed the body.'

'So soon? They said the police would come.'

'But then, you know what a clever man we have for our village headman, don't you?' said Lakshmi. 'The whole thing could be hushed up, he said. Of course you know what that means!'

It meant that the chief had demanded a bribe to hush things up.

Sabhesan came in through the back door and had his bath at the well. Lalita placed the sitting-plank and plate on the floor for him. He sat down, deep in thought, and ate silently. She wanted to share her grief with someone. She would have liked to tell him how she felt. But his expression was forbidding. She also remembered his anger over her help to Saroji.

After he had eaten, she asked tentatively, 'We must send some food for Sankaralinga Iyer's family, mustn't we? You know, they can't cook in a house of mourning.'

'Have you got any lunch prepared?'

'Yes.'

'Then why ask me? You've already been supplying them with raw rice. Now we can supply their food.'

Malicious! She controlled herself with difficulty.

She was trying to decide whether to send the food in spite of his sarcasm, when, to her relief, she heard him call out to someone outside. 'Kitta, we've cooked some food for them. Take it there.'

Sabhesan put on a fresh shirt and went out.

After sending the food, Lalita had her lunch and came and sat on the porch. Lakshmi sat down at the edge of the platform. 'So that's the end of Saroji,' she said. 'I doubt if those people will go to Madras,' she continued.

'Why not?'

'Who'll look after the children if they go there? Here they've at least got that woman of his.' Lakshmi burst out laughing. 'The things that happen in this village! It's all rather funny when you come to think of it!'

'No, it's not funny, Lakshmi.'

'Oh, well' said Lakshmi, 'You live up there in the clouds!'

CHAPTER FOURTEEN

Meenu was shocked when she heard the news that evening.

'So the women of this village have mustered enough courage at last,' she said. 'This death is a protest, manni. Rukmini protested by running away. This woman has protested in a more terrible way. How are you going to show your protest?'

Lalita started. 'What are you talking about, Meenu? I have nothing to do with these women.'

'Oh, sorry,' said Meenu, with a slight sneer. 'Of course, you have nothing to do with these women. I can understand them, but I can't understand you!'

Lalita smiled. 'You have to be a little older for that, Meenu.'

'I'm not sure. I don't think I'll ever be able to understand you, because you just don't belong to our times.'

'You speak as if Saroji did the proper thing in dying as she did. But it was a miserable death. It was done out of self-pity and anger with no thought of anything else.'

'I'm not seeking to justify it. But her death is understandable. If people aren't outraged or aggrieved, they can't ever be free. We have to feel indignant and show others that we are indignant. Otherwise, we are going to be slaves forever.'

'But indignation should not destroy. Think of what she has done. Has anything been gained by it? Nothing, except that the children have been orphaned.'

'But her husband is probably a different man because of her death.'

Lakshmi smiled wryly. 'What a child you are, Meenu! Do men like him ever change? He'll just say, 'Good riddance!''

Meenu sat on the floor for a while, her hands round her knees, a vacant stare in her eyes.

'What's the matter, Meenu?'

'The more I think of it, the more hopeless it all seems.'

'You shouldn't brood over these things.'

'I can't help it. This place makes me brood.'

'Didn't I tell you? This is an awful place!' exclaimed Lakshmi.

Lalita laughed. 'If we keep blaming the place and the people we can't hope for anything but sorrow and bitterness.'

'I do feel bitter, manni.'

'No, Meenu, don't let that happen to you! Once bitterness invades you, it corrupts your nature.'

'But I get angry only because I care for others. If you are not affected by what's happening around you, it can only mean that there's something wrong with you.'

Meenu accused her of being unconcerned, thought Lalita. To Meenu, anything unaccompanied by violent protest was a lack of concern. She couldn't probably imagine Lalita's shock that morning, her horror, her grief. And her anguish at those children's plight.

'I want to grip you by the shoulder and shake you up real hard!' That had been Meenu's refrain ever since she came here. How to make her understand that all these goings-on did not leave her unaffected? True, her reaction differed. She felt sad rather than angry. She felt depressed, rather than indignant.

If you think you can reform this society with your anger, you don't know the first thing about it!

It took Lalita some time to realise that Raju had joined them and was sitting with them. There was a new expression in his eyes. Sadness? Turbulence? Shock? All those together. It disturbed her.

'When did you come back from play, Raju?'

'I didn't want to play today.'

'Why?'

'How can I play when Gopu-Venkittu's mother is dead?'

I don't really know my son, she thought.

'Didn't I tell you manni? There's another Raju inside him.'

Raju was gazing into the distance. He seemed not to have heard them. Suddenly he blurted out, 'You know why Gopu's mother died, don't you?'

Lalita started. 'Why talk about all that, Raju?'

But Raju was not listening. 'They say Gopu's father used to beat her up badly. That's why she went and hanged herself like that.'

'Raju! How many times has Father told you not to discuss other people's affairs?' Lalita chided.

Raju hung his head. Presently he began again, 'Meenu akka, Saroji amma will be up there.'

'Where?'

'In the sky!'

'Who said so?'

'I know. Those who die go to God. And God is in the sky.'

'Perfect logic!'

Raju started vacantly again. 'If only we could go up to the skies! It must be so lovely up there. Don't you think so, Meenu akka?'

'Stop that nonsense,' said Meenu sharply.

Lalita felt her heart pounding. What makes this boy speak these words?

'Sitting here and chattering away at twilight time, are you? Are we going to have something to eat? Or has this become a house of mourning?' It was the familiar voice.

Lalita stood up instantly. 'A house of mourning'. It was a phrase she had been hearing often enough. But it made her cringe today.

'I've finished cooking. You can come and have your supper.' She spoke as always softly, as if she were impervious to provocation.

'It's study-time. But you are gossiping away. Are you going to hold a meeting over everything that happens in our Brahmin quarter?'

Meenu went into her room without a word. Raju's expression had changed to one of fear. He blinked foolishly, his mind fixed on but one idea – how to escape a thrashing.

'Get in, you wretch! Go, put on your shirt. You've been sitting all this while in the cold without a shirt on. If I see you sitting like that again I'll skin you alive!'

Raju vanished into Meenu's room.

Lalita laid the sitting plank and plate on the floor. Sabhesan ate in a mood of moroseness.

'If somebody is not affected by what's happening around him, it can only mean that there's something wrong with him!'

Lalita reined her thoughts in. Nothing would be gained by diagnosing his ailment. People don't really change. Nobody can change who stays within that charmed circle marked 'I'. You are born kind or you are not. It's like being born blind or dumb. It's possible now to cure blindness or deafness partially, but an unfeeling heart is incurable.

Suddenly Sabhesan's plate went flying through the air. It fell hitting the wall with a clang.

Lalita came back to earth with a bump. Sabhesan raged.

'I've asked twice for pickles and there you sit staring into space. What impudence!'

Lalita got up, flustered. 'I didn't hear you! Just a moment!'

Sabhesan jerked his hand free of rice and stood up. 'I don't want it. Eat it yourself! Sitting there as if possessed by some evil spirit! And then saying 'I didn't hear you!' It is nothing but play-acting. Every bit of it. There are ways and ways of showing indifference.'

The rice that he had mixed with buttermilk lay scattered on the floor. Desolate, Lalita looked at it with a new sort of misery.

'Please sit down. I swear that I didn't hear what you said.'

'I don't want to eat what you throw my way like a piece of bread to a dog.'

Sabhesan rushed to the well and washed his hands.

On an impulse she turned. There he was, Raju, at the kitchen door, looking steadily at her. The dread and the grief in that look made her recall what he had said a few minutes earlier. 'If only we could go to the skies! It must be so lovely up there!'

CHAPTER FIFTEEN

The bullock cart was waiting for her. Meenu readied herself for college.

'I am going to college, manni!' she cried.

'Bye! And be careful, my dear!'

As she climbed into the bullock cart, Meenu smiled at her manni's daily advice. It was doubtful if even her mother had shown such tender concern while speaking to her.

'Can I come with you in the cart, Meenu akka?' Raju pleaded. 'Father is not at home', he added by way of explanation.

She was sorry for him. 'All right. Get in, quick!'

His face brightened. He flung his bag into the cart and heaved himself in after it.

They began to move. The boy looked so happy. Why did her mama deny this boy his simple desires and pleasures?

'He must not go by cart. Once the body gets used to luxuries, it is unfit for any work.'

How solemn he was in putting his principles to practice!

If Raju asked him for something once in a while, the answer was invariably 'No!'

'Velu! Don't tell father that I came in the cart, please', Raju pleaded with the cart-man.

'Ah, but I am going to tell him!' teased Velu.

There was fear in Raju's eyes as he said, 'Then stop the cart. I'll get off!'

'Aiyaiye! Sit down! What a frightened goose you are! How long are you going to quake with fear like this?'

Meenu said nothing. She had been here for more than six months now, but she could feel no affection for her mama. Yet she was deeply attached to her manni who had no blood ties with her.

Sabhesan never had a good word for anyone. It was abuse, abuse all the time... Even when he was voicing his concern.

'Why didn't you have your Horlicks today?' 'Are you sitting there in the cold without a shirt on?' 'Sleeping without a pillow, are you?'

And every outburst was followed by violence.

Raju certainly couldn't be expected to love such a father. Nor could he ever realise that his father's anger proceeded for an exaggerated concern.

'Father doesn't love me at all!' He had been so sure.

They had reached his school. Raju slipped past Meenu and got off the cart with a joyous jump. Several boys had gathered to watch him arrive. He looked proudly at them.

'Look at the landlord coming by hooded cart!' Someone shouted.

Meenu watched him put up with the taunt.

'All right, Velu, get along! It's getting late for my college!' she cried.

'That boy is in mortal fear of his father, amma!'

Meenu looked at the fields. Green land and arid hearts!

People were poisoning the air they breathed with anger, jealousy, gossip, idleness. And all these were reflected in their children—in their stupidity, their loose talk, their meanness. Twenty years from now the village would be much, much worse.

These men and women were worms within their cocoons—unventilated cocoons, dwellings without windows. Blind worms that kept going round and round inside their cocoons gasping for air.

When she reached the college, she heard the bell. She ran up the steps and heard hurried footsteps follow her. She turned to look.

Hariharan!

He smiled.

'Good morning, sir!'

'Good morning. I think I've told you not to call me 'Sir'.'

'I can't remember...but I do remember that this is a college campus.'

'Even so, I don't like so much respect. I live on your street. We are not strangers.'

She blushed and laughed to conceal her embarrassment. Walking fast to keep up with him, she said, 'But it is not easy to feel that we live on the same street. I haven't met anyone else in your family.'

'No one in our house goes out.' He said thoughtfully. 'Why don't you come round to see us?'

She wondered if she had forced the invitation.

'Can you come this evening?' His eyes and smile betrayed his eagerness.

She said 'OK.', and walked away briskly, conscious that she was late for her class.

'Thank you. I'll expect you then!'

She entered the classroom, face flushed and heart pounding. She could not concentrate.

He had tried to close the gap between them during the past few months. He had stopped addressing her formally. Every time she met him, and looked into his smiling face, she felt alive and moved. Her eyes would mist over and her heart race. The more she thought about it, the more awkward she felt. Also, a bit ashamed.

Mere infatuation, she thought. She was perhaps attracted by his sophistication and his modern clothes that set him apart from all the other men in the village, with their country ways and orthodoxy.

He behaved naturally with her, much as he would have done in the city. If she had misunderstood his sociability and laughter in the midst of the closed society of the village, it was her fault.

If she were to give way to these impulses, what would happen to all her ideals and dreams?

She still cherished those ideals. She still felt furious when she saw a woman being bullied. Women suffered because they were weak. Because they were not economically independent. Because they had no knowledge of the world.

Take these men of the brahmin street, for example. They had driven Rukmini to adultery. They had driven Saroji to suicide. As for Lalita... her thoughts came to an abrupt halt.

She could not understand her Lalita manni. In spite of all that anger and abuse from Sabhesan, Lalita still managed to keep smiling. She went about like someone who did not know the meaning of discontent; had never been sick at heart. How she loved everyone, without distinction! She thought again of that scene when Lalita had stood before her with the earthen lamp in her hand. And again she felt that curious thrill.

My manni must have superhuman resources, thought Meenu. But, I am just an average woman. When I heard of Saroji's death that day, I was furious. I could have strangled Saroji's husband! And I wanted to shake up Lalita manni, too. I made up my mind then, that I would never get married.

Never shall I bend before an arrogant male to receive the tali round my neck. The marriage knot may turn into the hangman's noose. Never, never shall I give way to any weakness, I resolved.

But here I am, all a-flutter, just because a man with a fine set of teeth smiles at me like a film hero and promises to wait for me!

Ridiculous of me. Really!

She forced herself to listen to the lecture.

When she left for home that afternoon, she remembered her mother's letter. She got it only yesterday. So typical of her mother to write as she did, 'I just can't believe that you can live in that village. How do you spend your time? How are your lessons? Is it a passable college? You used to be so fretful even here in the city. What was it that attracted you in that sleepy village! Daddy and I are racking our brains for an answer! When can we expect you home?'

She smiled to herself. I myself can't explain it, yet, she told herself.

She had been waiting quite long for the bus home.

'You are Lalita's sister-in-law's daughter, aren't you?'

She turned, surprised. It was Rukmini with a faint smile on her face.

'Yes.'

'How do you come to be here?'

'I'm studying at this college.'

'I see. Come round to my place. I'm staying close by, in the next lane. Just take care not to mention your visit to anybody in the Brahmin quarter!'

She felt curiously affected by Rukmini's friendly smile.

'Some other time, mami. I haven't the time today.'

'All right.'

Rukmini looked round once and asked with some hesitation.

'How's Krishnan? Have you seen him?'

'He's fine, mami. I saw him playing yesterday.'

'I brought my second child—a girl—along with me, when I came to live with this man. But Krishnan was old enough to know about these things. So he refused to come. But I can't give him up so easily. The days I think of him, I just can't eat.'

The bus was not far off now.

'I'll come to see you again. That's one way I can find out about Krishnan! I'm so glad I met you, Meenu!'

Boarding the bus, Meenu waved to her before sitting down. The bus began to move. She turned and kept looking back and found Rukmini standing there for a long while, till she was finally lost in the distance.

She wondered if nature was anti-woman. How had society got tied up into so many knots?

That evening, after tiffin and coffee, she took Raju along to meet Hariharan. Before she could knock at the door, it flew open, and there he stood beaming on her! Forgotten were her ideals and resolutions. All her resistance seemed to evaporate. How good it was just to feel happy!

CHAPTER SIXTEEN

'Hello! Come in!' he said eagerly. He seemed rather effusive to Meenu. But it was an infectious effusiveness and made her smile in spite of herself.

She went in, holding Raju's hand.

It was bright inside, unlike most other houses in the street. It had a modern, well-scrubbed look. It was as quiet as if there were nobody at home.

'Sit down, Let me go in and fetch mother.'

Meenu looked round. There was a bookshelf near the sofa. About ten snaps in a single photo frame were that of Hariharan's sister Manju—it must be her—at different stages of life. As a baby of up to two years, her legs were visible. The later pictures were all half-length. Manju seemed determined not to smile after two. Her lips were tightly pressed and unsmiling in the later pictures.

'Welcome, my dear!'

Meenu turned to look.

A middle-aged woman had come in. She had Manju's features. But the expression was serene, affectionate.

'Namaskaram mami!'

'Namaskaramma. Do you like the college here?'

'It's okay. Not too bad. Much better than I had expected!'

'How can the college be bad, when I am a lecturer there?'

His mother smiled. She seemed to do everything deliberately.

Beside his exuberance, she seemed a model of serenity.

'How do you like this place, mami?'

'But how can one know anything about this place, unless one goes out?'

Meenu did not answer.

'Bring them something to eat, Mother, will you?'

So he wished to change the subject.

'No, please don't. We've just had our tiffin and coffee.'

'Have some fruit, then,' said Hariharan.

'I'll come back in a moment, Hari. You talk to her,' said the mother.

'Won't you sit down, Meenu?'

Suddenly, she was shy. Raju clinging to her, not knowing what to do, had already started mumbling 'Let's go home!'

Hariharan was looking at her, smiling.

'These photographs are all your sister's, aren't they?'

'Yes.' His face clouded over.

'Where is she now?'

'In there.'

'May I see her?'

He got up with some hesitation. 'She doesn't like meeting people.'

'But I'd like to make friends with her. It's rather hard in this place for me, with no girl my age to talk to.'

'It mayn't be enough for you to want to be friends with her,' he said wryly.

Hari's mother came back with a plate of bananas.

'Meenu wants to meet Manju, mother. Please take her in.' It was an order rather than a request.

After a moment's confusion, and a questioning look at him, his mother turned to Meenu and asked her to come with her.

The room next to the hall was curtained off. When the mother drew the curtain aside and went in, Manju, who had been staring at the rafters, gave a start.

She looked at Meenu as if assessing her. There was suspicion and resentment in her look. 'Don't meddle with me', it seemed to say.

'Manju, here's a neighbour, Meenu, come to see you. Meenu is studying at the town-college.'

Manju turned her head in a flash. 'You mean, the college where Anna teaches?'

'Yes.'

Manju was hostile. 'I don't want to meet anybody.' She said vehemently.

'But, Manju, I want to be friends with you!' said Meenu.

Manju screamed. 'Am I a museum piece? A leggy girl come to flaunt what she has and I haven't! Must be one of Anna's schemes to humiliate me. I don't need friends.'

Meenu was taken aback.

'Sorry Manju. I came on my own. No one brought me to you... The world is full of afflictions – blindness, mental reta...'

'Shut up and get out!'

Meenu went out. Hariharan, who had been looking out through the window, turned to face her.

'Sorry, Meenu. I warned you what it would be like.'

Meenu laughed briefly. 'It doesn't matter,' she said. 'Come on, Raju let's go.'

When they were out on the street, Raju asked, 'Are we going home, akka?'

'No, to the temple.'

'Then let me go and bring Lakshmi along.'

The three walked towards the temple. Meenu was lost in thought.

'Meenu, you went to that Aiyer's house, didn't you?'

Meenu laughed.

'What are you laughing at?'

'It's the way you refer to people here. One is always known by his caste in this place. You are determined to have fences.'

'But that's the custom here. I can't understand any other method.'

Meenu walked on silently.

'Whatever you may say, Meenu, we can never get rid of castes.'

'But, if we keep reminding ourselves about these divisions, they will live on forever, Lakshmi.'

'Why do you bother yourself with these things?' asked Lakshmi.

'But Lakshmi, it is a pity. We have so many problems—bigger, more important problems. We have found no solutions for hunger or disease. Look at how we keep fighting among ourselves in the name of caste.'

'But people have something called self-respect, don't they?'

'We were not born with self-respect. Only with hunger, Lakshmi!'

'What do I know about these things? You are learning about a lot of big things, and so you like to lecture.'

'It's not because I'm educated, Lakshmi. It's just that these things upset me. To bear with our natural misfortune is hard enough. Now just take that girl's case...'

She stopped abruptly.

'Which girl?'

'The girl we saw the other day in the temple – you know, the one in the wheel chair, Hariharan's sister. She can't walk, so she hates everybody, quarrels with everybody!'

'Why, what happened? I think you went there today!'

'I went to her room to meet her. But she shouted at me. Said she didn't want to meet anyone. So I came away.'

'That explains why no one ever comes out of that house—except that sami, of course.'

The green fields looked alluring. Raju was running about and laughing, trying to catch butterflies.

'I don't need anyone to be friends with me!'

The intense hatred in those eyes! As if she had made up her mind that no one could understand her. It was just possible that she was made to feel useless by the excessive concern shown her at home. She had become Nature's special victim. Didn't Hariharan sense this? Or, had he stopped trying to change her? She remembered what Hariharan had told her that day, that they were here mainly for her sake. But how could it benefit her to shut herself up in that dark room and never to see the world outside?

'Look here, Meenu akka!'

There was a yellow-and-black butterfly struggling between Raju's fingers.

'Aiyaiyo! Let it go!'

'It feels soft as silk, Meenu akka!'

'Poor thing, let it go. If the wings break, it won't be able to fly.'

Raju opened out his fingers and let it fly away.

'Then it may have to sit on a wheel chair like that girl we saw? Isn't that so, akka?'

Meenu looked at him, startled. The surprising things that this simple-minded boy came out with! 'But don't make fun of anyone Raju.'

They went round the temple corridor hand-in-hand. There were people in the temple today. They could hear loud voices.

'None can match our Sabhesan in money matters. You know what he's done, don't you?'

'Of course, I know. He's a mean minded fellow, for all his wealth!'

Meenu dragged Raju out.

'Come, let's go out and have a look,' she said.

CHAPTER SEVENTEEN

'I saw some parrots flying. Let's look for them, Raju!' said Meenu.

'Where akka?'

'There! That's where they went. Walk along and see.'

Lakshmi was some distance away walking slowly towards them. Meenu hoped that the conversation in the temple would be over before she reached them. She could hear it quite clearly from out there.

'He got Sankaralinga Iyer's land dirt-cheap. The fool sold it to Sabhesan at half-price and now he's in a fix. His son, Nana, has also woken up now. His wife is dead and their plan of going to Madras has been dropped.'

'What is he going to do now?'

'He wants to buy back at least a part of his land.'

'But Sabhesan won't agree to sell it back, will he?'

'Worse than that. Sabhesan is willing to sell the land back all right. But at the market-rate, not what he bought it for.'

'Well done! He and Nana grew up together. They've known each other all their lives. All that doesn't mean a thing now, I suppose?'

'Who remembers all that when it comes to money?'

'That's why God has given him a nitwit for a son!'

'True. The boy hasn't got the father's brains.'

'The harm you do to others comes right back to you and with interest!'

Meenu felt herself shiver. Lakshmi had arrived.

'Didn't you go round the temple? Why are you standing here?'

'I'm just waiting for you. Raju went after the parrots.' She spoke loudly, and the voice from the inner corridor stopped abruptly.

The temple priest came out with another man. He beamed at her.

'Why Meenu! I haven't seen you for a long time now. Having your exams, perhaps?'

'Yes. Won't you recommend me to your goddess?'

The priest laughed.

'Why should I, when you are here in person? A clever girl! And Sabhesan's niece, not just a nobody!'

Raju came running and said, gasping for breath, 'No parrots there, Meenu akka!'

'Never mind! We'll see a lot of them on our way back.'

When the priest waved the lighted camphor round the devi, Raju patted his cheeks in the ritual gesture of submission and devotion. Meenu smiled at him.

'What's your prayer, Meenu akka?'

'That Raju should be happy!'

Raju gave Lakshmi a shy smile.

The priest handed him the holy ashes. 'Here, take this. May your fate be a good one!'

Meenu was annoyed by the remark, his disparaging comments of a few minutes ago still rankling in her mind.

The sight of the boy, with those stripes of holy ash on his forehead, brought on a swell of pity. When the three of them were about to leave the temple, she could see that the priest and the two men were speaking in hushed tones and laughing.

On the way back, Meenu's thoughts were of her mama. If what she had heard was true, it was despicable. Her mama was one of the few hard working people in this village—he never wasted his time. But he was acquisitive. For whose sake? He wouldn't even buy a pressure-cooker to lighten Lalita's load of cooking on the firewood stove. He didn't have a kind word for his son. Nor did he give him the comforts enjoyed by even children of poor parents.

All his wealth was not designed to increase the comfort or happiness of anyone in the family. It was a symbol of power and masculinity. He felt he could crush everyone with his money-power.

How different Lalita manni was! Why are such couples yoked in marriage?

They had reached the Brahmin-quarter. There was only one woman now on the front-platform of Sankaralinga Iyer's house – Saroji's rival. Saroji's two sons, Venkittu and Gopu, were playing with tops on the street. Everyone in the street looked dismal.

Those children playing there in their dusty shirts and shorts—how could Sabhesan have the heart to deprive them of their due?

But then, Sabhesan was a stranger to all the finer impulses of the human heart. He would say he was not responsible for others' stupidity. 'Why should I be indulgent to a fellow who is so self-indulgent?' In all the years he had spent with Lalita manni, could he not have changed, loosened up a little bit? But without any closeness, how was change possible?

He doesn't know anything about manni—what a treasure she is. Her nobility, her spirituality—these are things beyond his comprehension. For him she is just a woman—someone to be ruled by man!

She was getting angrier by the day with her uncle. But all her indignation was not going to achieve anything. He must wish for a change in himself.

Balu teacher's son, Krishnan was seen playing in front of his house, all by himself, as always. It was as though he were bound to the place by some oath. The sight brought back thoughts of his mother Rukmini—her tears and her sorrow.

'The days I think of him, I just can't eat.' She had said.

This boy with his troubled look and dark ringed eyes must also be thinking of his mother. She stopped by the house and asked him with a smile, 'How are you, Krishnan?'

He smiled shyly, 'Fine!'

'Why don't you come to our place? You can play with Raju.'

Krishnan didn't reply. Her question seemed to embarrass him.

Raju dragged him by the hand.

'Yes, Krishnan. Why don't you come to my house?'

'But I can't. I can't leave the house open.'

'You mean your father is not at home?' asked Meenu shocked.

Krishnan hung down his head 'No.'

'I know. His father is playing cards on the river bank with that Nana mama.' Said Raju.

'Hush, Raju! Come on, let's go home!'

But Raju missed the warning in her voice and nodded his head vigorously. He said with a laugh, 'I know, I have seem them at it!'

'All right! Let's go now! Krishnan, you can come over when your father is at home. Come and have lunch with us when you have a holiday next, will you?'

Krishnan seemed to be looking for something in the sky. He did not reply.

'My mother makes cheppan kizhangu fry, so nice and crisp. Why don't you come?' asked Raju.

Krishnan's face broke into a smile of superior wisdom indicating that he was no longer a child like Raju.

'Have you cooked dinner, Krishnan?'

Even as she asked the question, Meenu chided herself for her lack of good manners.

'Not yet. Father will come and he'll cook. But if he doesn't come soon I'll eat yesterday's rice and go to sleep.'

'Aiyaiyo! You'll catch a cold if you eat cold rice at night!' cried Raju.

'Let's go, Raju!'

As she walked on, Meenu felt those two dark-ringed eyes piercing her back. She felt infinitely sad. Lakshmi too was silent.

Meenu sat down on the porch, with her hands round her knees. Twilight was giving way to darkness. In a few minutes it would be dark. Lalita's soft singing came to her:

Engenge pathalum ev vuyirukkum Av vuyirai ...

Wherever I turn to look, O Lord!

It is Thee I see.

Thou art the life in all living things!

Shed Thy grace on me, O Lord!

That I may treat every living being with compassion

As though the life it bears is my own.

Lalita manni doesn't really need to pray for this grace, Meenu said to herself. She's born with it.

She had been deeply affected by Krishnan's plight. His taciturn looks showed maturity and responsibility. The way he sat there all day! He had taken over his mother's role, to look after the house. What did he think of his mother? Did he hate her?

... I shall treat every living being with compassion as though the life it bears is my own...

Meenu stood up suddenly.

'Raju! Get inside. Quick! Mama is coming!'

Like a shot, Raju darted in. He didn't even turn to look back.

As Sabhesan reached home, his face flashed with fury.

Meenu was engulfed by a sudden wave of anger. She must ask him today, she must.

Put him in the dock. Grill him with questions.

CHAPTER EIGHTEEN

Meenu stepped down from the platform.

Sabhesan was disconcerted at finding her still standing there, not retreating at his approach. He looked at her steadily as he climbed the steps.

'How many times have I told you not to sit out on the porch after dark? Get in!'

'But this is the only place where there's any breeze!'

She watched him casually as the purple glow of anger spread over his face.

'The breeze inside is good enough for you. Get in.'

The words were a whip. The sight of Raju standing inside the house, his eyes wide with fear, the consciousness that Sabhesan's raised voice could be heard till the last house in the street, made her leave.

Sabhesan waited till she entered her room, then went quickly to the swing in the hall and sat down on it.

'You there! Blinking like a sheep-thief! That's all you ever do! Go in!'

Raju hurried into Meenu's room and sat down close to the wall, his satchel beside him.

'Now, take out your books and read! Are you a son of mine! Will you ever get past the tenth class? Or will you hang round my neck all your life?'

Meenu opened her book, watching Raju's panicky face and trembling limbs.

'You've all ganged up against me. Going visiting, house after house! Roaming round the village, saying you're going for a walk! Sitting like a prostitute on the porch after dark because you must have fresh air! You call yourselves women, don't you?' How had he found out where she had been to, wondered Meenu. Did he have spies?

She stood up.

Ignoring Raju's frightened look she went to the hall. 'We are all women, mama! Have no doubts about it!'

Sabhesan seemed to find it unbelievable that anyone would dare to answer him. Glowering, he said, 'Women ought to behave like women.'

'You mean we ought all to be like manni? Cowering before you and listening to all your abuse with never a word in reply!'

'Shut up, you cheeky twit! If you want to stay here you've got to listen to me and behave. Or else leave for Madras, bag and baggage!'

Meenu felt suddenly defeated and was silent. So that was his weapon! He would use it every time she stood up to him!

'Meenu akka, please come in!' Hearing the whispered words so near her, Meenu turned and found Raju behind her, pulling her plaited hair. The beseeching look in his eyes made her comply with his wishes.

When she opened her book again, she was unable to concentrate. Her anger had achieved nothing. She had really been impudent. Why did she talk back like that? Not even her mother would have spoken to him so. The anger had been smouldering within her all evening. Perhaps it was the picture of those two children playing in the dust that had triggered it. Anyway, why could she not just be quiet?

She reined her thoughts in and looked at Raju, earnestly scanning a book. His thoughts were certainly far, far away. How could her mama expect him to pass the tenth at this rate? Again, she forced herself to study.

'Won't you come and have your dinner, now?' Lalita asked Sabhesan.

'I don't want any dinner. For all the respect I get in this house.'

'Oh, she's only a child. Please don't mind what she said.'

'I know what to mind and what not to. So you think you're qualified to advise me. Do you?'

'Siva, Siva! Who is to advise whom? You just imagine that no one respects you. If you don't eat, the rest of us won't feel like eating either.'

'So that's it! I have to stuff myself with something so that you people can eat. Cold rice and buttermilk will do for me.'

Meenu wiped her forehead hard. It was a wonder that Lalita manni had not gone mad. As for herself, a whole year's stay in this place would certainly drive her mad. How was she going to complete the course?

'I said I wanted cold rice. Why are you serving me hot rice?'

'There's no cold rice left.'

'Why! A stone-bowl full of it was left over this afternoon, I know.'

'It's all finished.'

'But how?'

'I'm asking you! Why don't you answer?'

'Saroji's children had come. They were hungry…so…'

'And so you, the Annapurani – the Goddess of Plenty, that you are – had of course to feed them! At this rate, this house is never going to prosper. Never! With your prodigal ways, you will make a pauper of the richest man! Here I am, saving bit by tiny bit like a sparrow. And there you go, throwing things out of the back door. You seem to care more for those children than their father Nana ever does. What do you have to do with that drunkard?'

Meenu felt utterly shaken, hearing those words.

He calls himself a man! There was no limit to the man's arrogance!

Someone was at the door. Meenu turned to look, and found Lalita there. With a smile on her lips and a tender look in her eyes. No trace of the battlefield she had left behind. Meenu felt a sudden spurt of anger. Manni doesn't seem to have any self-respect at all, she thought.

'Both of you can come and eat now.'

'Has mama finished eating?'

'Yes, and Raju, get up!'

'Where's Father?'

'He's sitting on the front porch.'

Raju got up swiftly. Meenu followed. Unable to detect any change in Lalita's expression, Meenu wondered if she knew about Sabhesan's conditions for returning his lands to Sankaralinga Iyer. Maybe, she did know everything, and that was why she was feeding those children. Perhaps she gave up trying to reform Sabhesan because she knew it was impossible.

'Meenu akka?' Raju called her softly.

'Yes?'

'I'll tell Krishnan not to come to eat with us.'

'Why?'

'Father will get angry.'

Lalita's eyes met Meenu's for a moment, then looked down.

'We shouldn't tell anyone not to come to our house, Raju.'

'But if I invite him, he'll come. And you'll give him things to eat. Then father will get cross with you...'

'Don't worry about all that, Raju.'

Raju looked at her in some confusion, then bent his head. He asked in a whisper, 'Amma, will you make some crisp cheppan kizhangu fry tomorrow? I'll take it to Krishnan when Father's not here. I can take it through the back door after Father leaves for the fields. Can't I?'

Lalita agreed.

When Raju had gone to bed, Meenu helped Lalita to clean the kitchen. After debating the point with herself for some time, she finally told Lalita what she had heard in the temple. But, watching Lalita's reaction she hastened to add, 'It was just loose talk, manni.'

Lalita said nothing. Only after they finished the work and bolted the kitchen door, did she look at Meenu. In a low voice she said, 'Meenu! Don't fret about these things. Go to bed. I'll sit up for a while in the courtyard.'

'Let me sit with you, then.'

'No. I want to be by myself for some time...'

'Then tell me tomorrow how many stars there are in the sky, will you?'

Lalita laughed. 'Yes, I will!'

It was with great difficulty that Meenu managed to drag her mind back to her books. After finishing her work, she lay down to sleep. As she drifted into sleep, she woke with a start. She could hear her mama's voice bellowing from the hall.

'Go away! You Goddess of Misfortune! How dare you advise me! Go away for good, like that woman – Nana's wife! And don't go alone. Take that wonderful son you've borne me along with you!'

CHAPTER NINETEEN

Meenu walked round the kolam pattern taking care not to step on it, and climbed into the cart that was waiting for her.

'Bye and be careful, Meenu!'

She looked out of the cart and waved to her manni. Lalita was standing just within the doorstep, a smile on her lips, as always.

Through her tears (she cried so easily these days), Meenu could see Hariharan cleaning his car. He might have been smiling at her. She withdrew into the cart. As she tried to suppress her tears, she wondered at her weakness. Then she realised that it was not weakness. Something had happened to her. It was the shock of sudden maturity that had brought on those tears. In Madras she had been a butterfly, silly, uninvolved.

What a lot of things she had learnt since she came here, from these houses of a single street! 'This is life!' they seemed to tell her, 'and if you can understand us, you'll understand life!'

Whenever she thought of the miseries within these houses she felt pity well up in her heart.

'Go away for good, like that woman – Nana's wife!' Those had been Sabhesan's words last night.

She looked at the fields on both sides of the road. She was troubled.

How did her manni manage to be cheerful this morning after all that?

Could it be that her mama had made up with her later? He was not the sort to make up, though.

No. It must have been Lalita manni who had made her peace with herself, attributing everything to what she called ignorance.

Meenu could not concentrate on her studies that day. The words kept reverberating in her ears: 'Go away for good!'

When her classes were over, she went to the library. As she ran her eyes over the shelves, a title caught her – Helen Keller's autobiography. She pulled it out, took one more book, and was just out of the library, when she met Hariharan.

'Hello!' he beamed at her.

'Hello! Think of the Devil... they say!'

'And here I am!' said Hariharan.

How readily he laughed! Well, she used to be like that too, a few months ago.

'But what made you think of me?'

'I just came across this book here. I wonder if Manju would read it...'

He took it from her and browsed through it.

'Thanks, Meenu. But Manju won't touch it!' His face seemed to cloud over.

'Why?'

'She takes everything amiss. And she's quite determined not to do anything that we suggest.'

Meenu said, 'You needn't tell her anything. Just leave the book in a likely place and see if she picks it up...'

He looked touched.

'Thanks a lot for the interest you show in my sister, Meenu!'

She felt slightly vexed, as if he had somehow underestimated her.

'But it is quite natural for anyone to take an interest in her.'

'It's just that people seem to have forgotten how to be natural!'

'Thank you. Let's see if she reads it.'

In the college compound, there stood a tamarind tree. A group of men-students had collected under it. She had noticed the group there every day. They made snide remarks as she went by. What fools they were, if they gathered there just to see her pass!

Did they gain confidence only as a group? Not a single young man had so far spoken to her directly or naturally.

As she passed the gate the group burst into raucous laughter.

'Hey! No! Don't say that! People of her caste will come after you!'

'Let them come! We'll prove what rogues we are! Times have changed, brother!'

It was infuriating. She would have liked to go back and fight them. But no! She controlled herself and walked faster.

Times would never change, if this was the way our youngsters' thoughts were conditioned. Mere parrots with no minds of their own. People were not people for them. Just castes.

She was indignant. Was this to be our fate for ages to come?

Anyway, why was it that everything that she saw or heard made her sadder than usual today?

'Meenu!'

It was Rukmini. She had a packet in her hand and was smiling hesitantly. 'I have been waiting for you. Did you see Krishnan after that day?'

'Yes, I did.'

'Is he all right?'

'Oh, quite.'

'Will you do me a favour, Meenu? Krishnan is very fond of thool pakoda. But so long as I was with them, there never was enough to cook such things. I have made some today. Will you take it to him? And please don't misunderstand.'

Meenu laughed. 'Why should I misunderstand you mami? I'll certainly take it to him.'

'Let no one know about it.'

'Okay.'

It was pathetic to watch that wrinkled face brighten.

The smell of onions and oil went with her the whole way home. To her embarrassment, she found everyone in the bus covertly looking at her.

When she went past Lalita at the doorway, she heard her say, 'Why! You smell of pakoda!'

'Wait!' laughed Meenu, 'And I'll tell you all about it. But, first, let me have something to eat. I'm terribly hungry. The smell of this pakoda has made me hungrier than ever.'

'I've made some dosas. Come along.'

Meenu went to the well at the back and, under the shade of the portia tree, drew pot after pot of cool well-water and splashed it over her face. She began to feel better.

Eating the dosas, Meenu told Lalita about Rukmini. Lalita said slowly, 'Such a thing as that has to be done stealthily in this place!'

'Yes, I know. I'll go and give it to Krishnan. He'd be playing by himself.'

'Poor thing!'

'Who, manni?'

Lalita was looking at the sky through the window.

'Well, we're all 'poor things' one way or other!'

Meenu fell silent remembering all that she had heard last night. 'Let me go now, manni.' She said softly and went out with Rukmini's parcel.

Raju was out, playing. Her mama had not yet returned. Luckily even Lakshmi was nowhere to be seen.

Meenu walked fast. As usual, Krishnan was alone, playing with his marbles. On seeing her he rose, smiling hesitantly.

Meenu handed the packet to him and said: 'Here, eat this.'

'What's that?' He put out his hand.

'It's thool pakoda. It seems you like it very much!'

There was a faint smile on his lips now.

'Who told you?'

'Your mother!'

At once his face hardened. He withdrew his hand. She bent towards him and said affectionately: 'Take it Krishnan. I won't tell anyone. I met your mother in town. It's she who gave it to me. Take it!'

He did not say anything, just looked steadily at her. That look troubled her. He is no longer a child of ten, she thought. Must be at least twice his age, the way those eyes flashed. Savagely, he snatched the packet from her and flung it far into the street.

CHAPTER TWENTY

Meenu looked at Krishnan, astounded. The determined look in his eyes and the heaving of his small shoulders ruled out any questions. 'It would be foolish of you,' they seemed to say, 'to ask me why I did so.'

She stood looking at him. He turned away from her. He may break down if I asked him anything, thought Meenu. Suddenly, he darted into the house and shut the door on her. That gave her a jolt.

Menu stood staring at the closed door. How madly angry he was with Rukmini! Her desertion must have been traumatic. How intensely he must have felt her rejection, for him to fling her gift away like that! And he, a hungry child, who had not had a full meal for months, perhaps.

But then, he was no longer a child. That single action of his mother's had weighed him down with years. What he had done just now was not the reaction of a child. It was a clear act of repudiation. The woman who had abandoned him, was being rejected.

'Whom do you want?'

Meenu turned to look at the questioner. It was Ganesan's wife, Neelu. An atrocious gossip monger. Better be careful.

'Oh, I just came to see Krishnan.'

'Why?'

'Nothing special. Just thought I'd ask him to come to play with Raju. You know, Krishnan plays by himself all the time.'

Neelu laughed. 'Do you think he'll come with you? He's sitting there like a hen on its eggs. Perhaps he's afraid the house will run off like his mother!'

Meenu was annoyed. Neelu stood there, a naked child on her hip. Two of her older children were playing in the dust on the street. Two more were on the front pial of her house. Neelu's whole life was spent inside the house or on the front pial. Gossip was her mainstay, her pastime, her weapon.

Meenu stepped down and began to walk along the street. Neelu walked with her.

'How's your college?'

'Fine.'

Neelu's daughter, Padma, who must have been about sixteen, stood in the doorway, watching the street. Meenu had never seen her out on the street.

'Aren't you sending your daughter to school?'

Neelu gave a supercilious smile.

'So you think we'll send a grown-up girl out? Not we. Our people are strict in these matters.'

Meenu looked at Padma. There was an impatient eagerness in the girl's eyes.

'What can she do at home the whole day?'

'She reads magazines. She looks after the house and her younger brothers and sisters. There is enough work in any home. Why should she do anything else?'

Meenu walked on, smiling. She was sorry for the girl. A few more years, and Padma would be like her mother, a child on her hip, another in her womb and a few more on the dusty street. She too might look complacently at a 'grown-up' daughter peeping eagerly at the street from within her house. She too would walk round, wearing a supercilious smile.

'That Hariharan seems to be your teacher. Is he?'

'No. I've not taken his subject.'

'What does that mean?'

'He does not teach my class.'

'I see!' It was obvious that Neelu wanted to prolong the conversation. With a sardonic grin she continued, 'Padma says that fellow does not look like a teacher at all. He's more like a film-star.'

'I've got to go', said Meenu.

'Come to our place some time, Meenu. Or don't you like to visit the likes of us?'

'Oh, it's just that I haven't much time.'

Neelu's face still wore a mocking look.

As she walked home fast, Meenu could feel Neelu's grin piercing her back.

What Neelu had said made her laugh—'That fellow does not look like a teacher at all!' These people expected every teacher to look like their local school teacher, Balu Vadyar.

They wouldn't ever have understood what made Rukmini leave her husband. Ah, Rukmini!

What was she to tell Rukmini if she met her? If she came to her with a smile lighting up her wrinkled face and asked, 'Did my son eat the pakoda?...'

Lalita was waiting for her at the porch.

'Did you give him the pakoda? Meenu? What did he say?'

'When I told him it was from his mother, he didn't even bother to look inside the packet. He flung it on the street.'

'What?' Lalita looked pained. When she spoke again it was as if to herself, 'Children nowadays seem so proud. They are so quick to take offence and...'

'Bu that's as it should be, manni.'

'But I feel so uneasy, so afraid!'

'Krishnan will be all right, though. He is angry only because he knows how to think things through. That's why he's angry.'

Lalita laughed softly. 'Are all hot-tempered people blessed with this power of thought, Meenu?'

Meenu climbed on to the front platform and sat down in silence.

You should be angry about the right things. Otherwise, your mind could be twisted by anger. That's what had happened with Sabhesan mama and Manju.

Would Hariharan have given that book to Manju by now?

Raju came running. 'Meenu akka, come let's go to the temple.'

'No. Not today.'

'Please come. There's some special puja, it seems.'

'Is that so, manni?'

'I don't know. Anyway, why don't you go? But be back soon, before your mama returns.'

'Okay, bye.'

They could not find Lakshmi, so Meenu left with Raju. Raju kept up a ceaseless prattle. He chased butterflies and laughed when he came upon the storks, but nothing seemed to interest Meenu today.

Hearing approaching footsteps from behind, Meenu moved aside to give way.

'Don't you ever look about you when you walk?'

Hariharan's voice made her heart beat fast. He must have started after seeing her on her way. The thought was enough to make her blush. She looked at him, smiling.

'Of course, I do look around. But then, I'm not much bothered about people. I watch the trees and the birds...'

'How fortunate they are!'

Meenu burst out laughing. 'That girl was right, after all!'

'Which girl?'

'Ganesan's daughter, Padma.'

'What did she say?'

'That you don't look like a teacher at all, rather like a film star. Your speech sounds like something out of a film too!'

He laughed. 'A lovely girl in this beautiful setting of lush green fields has inspired the poet in me, Meenu!'

'You're a Botany lecturer, aren't you?'

'But I wish I were an English lecturer.'

'What for?'

'Then I could have taught you in college.'

She heard the warning signal within, He is going too far. She pulled herself together.

'That's funny. Here I am, thanking my stars that I didn't choose Botany. Otherwise, by now you'd have found out what a stupid girl I am!'

'Meenu akka, Look! Look! The storks!'

'Here I come!' Meenu ran off, glad of the excuse.

The storks darted off at their approach. Raju watched them fly with a look of rapture.

'Come on, Raju. Let's go to the temple. We'll find the parrots there.'

'Right. Let's run. Shall we?'

'Yes!'

She ran with him as if she were a little girl. The gloom of the last two days seemed suddenly to have lifted. She was aware that the interest Hariharan had shown in her had caused this shift in her mood and shyly acknowledged it.

There was no special worship in the temple as Raju had imagined. Even the priest was not to be seen anywhere. Goddess Panaiyatha stood alone, unattended. Meenu went chasing Raju round the corridor in gay abandon.

As she turned a corner, she ran straight into Hariharan who was coming in from the opposite direction.

'You seem to be doing this on purpose! Coming from the wrong side, in front of me!'

'But Meenu, it is you who are avoiding me, I think. Am I right?'

His mocking eyes and lips seemed very near. His hands held her waist in a tight grip.

CHAPTER TWENTY-ONE

Meenu felt a sudden warmth leap up within her. Her mind warned her, defying her to free herself from his grasp. But her heart and body stood helpless.

'Why, Meenu, what are you afraid of?'

His voice sounded soft and intoxicating. She felt his warmth spread through her. Controlling herself with an effort, she removed his hands.

'I'm afraid of myself,' she thought. But aloud she said: 'I'm afraid of Botany and Biology!' and smiled at him.

He laughed.

'That's why you've chosen History. What makes you think Biology now?'

'If I forget my Biology I'll be creating history in this village – something to keep their tongues wagging!'

'Why, Meenu! You have a way with words, sure. How old are you? At least thirty-eight, I imagine!'

'Minus about twenty!'

He drew nearer. She gave a slight start. He seemed to have lost all thought of his surroundings, was losing control of himself.

'Smart people are not bothered by wagging tongues, Meenu!'

'My mama will pack me off to Madras tomorrow!'

'Oh, will he? In that case, of course, it is wise to be careful. But why don't you change over to Botany? What's the good of History?'

She laughed. 'Sorry. I'm not interested in Botany.'

'What a pity?' he said with a grimace. 'Well then. At least keep coming to the library and read a lot of books, will you?'

She laughed again. 'I will! Now… where's Raju gone? Let me go and look for him.' She came out of the temple.

There stood Raju whistling through cupped hands. 'Koo-koo! Koo-oo!'

On seeing her, he smiled. He was transformed the moment he stepped out of the house, thought Meenu. Those twinkling eyes, this joyful face!

Was this the real Raju? Or the one crying before his father with terrified eyes and a dismal face?

'Meenu akka! Listen! The bird's answering my call!'

'Koo-oo! Koo-oo!', came a voice from the trees in the grove.

'Did you hear that, akka?'

'Yes. But we'll be late if you keep talking to the bird. Mama hates us to be late!'

His face fell, instantly.

'Well, we must go, then,' he conceded reluctantly. 'Didn't you go inside the temple yet, akka?'

'You can go now, but come back soon. There's no special puja, no priest even...Hurry!'

As Raju rushed in Hariharan came out smiling. Then he said, 'I won't keep you any longer. Don't worry! Just remember the library!'

Then he walked away fast. She felt like laughing. Was he just being cheeky? What would all this lead to?

'Let's go now, akka!'

Raju stood before her, sacred ash and kumkum covering his forehead.

'Shall we run now?'

'Yes, let's!'

But she could not laugh as before, when she ran. She was conscious of a new troubled furtiveness in herself. They ran past Hariharan and stopped for a brief rest only when they entered the village limits.

The card-playing group had collected on the platform at Sankaralinga Iyer's porch. The teacher, Balu Vadyar was among them, Meenu noted. She walked as fast as she could, holding Raju's hand. She heard their comments nevertheless, 'There goes the young landlord!'

'Thank God, he doesn't take after his father!'

'Just wait ten years. He'll go one better than his father!'

'Not possible! It calls for a special talent!'

Raju was walking along unconcerned, gazing up at the sky.

Well, how was he going to shape, she wondered.

Will he manage to look after all that his father has accumulated? This boy, who chats with the cuckoo, chases storks and butterflies and dreams of homes in the heavens! What is he going to be!

'I can take it through the backdoor after father leaves for the fields, can't I?'

That's what he will do. Fling all his money away, like seed scattered for birds to eat.

'Thank God! Father is not back, Meenu akka!'

'How can you tell?'

'Because mother is sitting out on the porch!'

'Does Sabhesan mama know anything, anything at all, about this boy except that he is not clever?' wondered Meenu sadly.

Lalita was indeed sitting there with her habitual smile. When she saw them her face lighted up. The thought of Hariharan came unbeckoned to Meenu and she felt her cheeks flushing.

'What happened today? Something new has happened – I see it in your face.'

Meenu was startled. 'What do you see there?'

'I can't explain it. But there's a new happiness in your face!'

Meenu was taken aback. Am I as transparent as that? She wondered. 'We came back running through the fields, Raju and I. I felt as though I had become a child again!'

Lalita stood watching her for a few moments as if she did not quite believe what she had said.

'Let's go in, Meenu. And Raju, go wash your hands and feet, say your prayers, and then sit down with your studies.'

Meenu got up. Raju went to the well to wash his feet and then entered the prayer room. Meenu stood strangely moved, watching him as he stood there, his eyes closed in prayer.

When Meenu went to the rear of the house to wash her feet, she found Lalita sitting on the platform at the back.

'What is it, manni?'

'Come here, I've got something to tell you!'

'What's the matter?'

'Your mama has given those lands back to Sankaralinga Iyer.'

Meenu looked surprised.

'How come?'

'They seem to have threatened to take the matter to our Village Council. Anyhow, he has now sold it back for the same price for which he bought it.'

So that explained the high spirits of the card-party at Sankaralinga Iyer's porch. Their conversation seemed to indicate that they had not yet forgiven Sabhesan mama. Or were they so arrogant because they had managed to retrieve their land?

'I feel so relieved now, Meenu. I've been miserable ever since you told me about the deal.'

Meenu took time to recover from her surprise. What could have made him change his mind? Fear of the village panchayat? The effect of Lalita manni's advice?

'It's really surprising, manni. I don't think mama would have done it for fear of the Village Council. You must have made him change his mind.'

Lalita glanced up at her. How much did she really know? Then she laughed softly.

'I don't think I can change his mind, ever. God must have done it. I can only pray. I have no right to do anything else.'

Didn't this manni of hers feel any anger or disgust towards her husband, wondered Meenu. Or was she as afraid of Sabhesan as Raju? There was no fear on Lalita's face. Nor was it a face of sheer helplessness.

'It's indeed a good thing that mama has returned their lands, manni. But I wonder how that Nana is going to manage this property. There's a big card-party going on at their house just now!'

Lalita's face clouded over. 'Only God can grant them wisdom, Meenu. There is nothing you and I can do for them. If this had not happened, our guilt and shame would have been unbelievable. Thank God we've been saved...'

Meenu went in to study.

Even Lalita's God seemed to be a peaceful being, never provoked to anger. But a peaceful approach to life would produce no results with men such as these. What was needed was a whip. Nothing less.

When she got to the college next morning, she was assailed by a sudden flood of memories. It was as if she could still feel the warmth of Hariharan's hands on her waist.

She pulled herself up. 'What on earth is the matter with me?'

Her attention wandered. That look, that smile and that clasp... and 'Just remember the library!'

She waited eagerly for the bell to ring, and left for the library, smiling to herself.

She certainly needed a book. Quite an important book.

The library looked deserted. Hariharan was seated in the Librarian's chair. He grinned cheerfully.

'The librarian has surrendered his place temporarily to me. May I help you?'

The moment she saw that mocking smile, Meenu realised that it was no longer possible to deceive herself.

CHAPTER TWENTY-TWO

He has probably sent the librarian out himself, thought Meenu, looking at his playful eyes.

'Thanks, but I'd like to choose the book myself,' she said.

He got up. 'Why do it all alone when I'm here to help? There are quite a lot of books to choose from!' He shadowed her as she waked away.

'Please don't trouble yourself,' said Meenu.

'But Meenu, perhaps I'm in your way?'

'Do let me go on, please,' Meenu begged. 'Somebody might see us'.

'Before anybody can see us, let me tell you something!'

'No, I don't want to know anything!'

She walked purposefully towards the shelves.

'As if there was another soul in this place that cared about the library,' he continued. 'You may be sure that you and I are the only ones who ever come here!'

Meenu made a pretence of looking for a book. But her heart was racing, her cheeks were warm. When she lifter her hand up to the top shelf, he caught her hand and said, 'I must tell you this—just that you look beautiful today!'

She withdrew her hand.

'It is not proper for a lecturer to say such things to a student, Mr. Hariharan!'

His face fell.

'Oh! Meenu, please don't get me wrong. I didn't mean to say anything improper. I'm only trying to tell you how close I feel to you. It's something I have felt for a long time now. You are not my student, are you? Anyway, is there any rule that forbids me to love my student?'

'Please don't confuse me. I don't believe in this stuff about 'love' and all that.'

He took her hand again and said, 'I'll make you believe in it, Meenu!'

Torn between what others would say and what she herself felt, she heard him.

'This is not a flirtation, Meenu. Do believe me, no woman has ever filled my heart so!'

There was a rustle behind and they turned round. Balu-teacher in their college library! How come?

Hariharan moved away at once and with a familiar laugh cried, 'Hello, namaskaram. So what brings you here?'

Balu did not look straight at them.

'Where's the librarian?' he asked.

'He's gone out. Tell me, what do you want?'

'He had promised me a book. I'll come tomorrow for it,' said Balu.

He walked away fast, not once glancing back. Meenu's eyes were wide with fear.

Hariharan looked tenderly at her and laughed. 'Why do you look like that, Meenu?'

Meenu left the library in silence, and walked towards her class, upset and somewhat panicky. When she reached her class and sat down, her hands were trembling.

This Balu-teacher would now go round with a tom-tom to spread the news of what he had seen, fleshing it out with imaginary details. The whole Brahmin-quarter would soon be agog with a full-fledged scandal. She did not know much about him but could not expect anything better from such as him. He would not be silent during those daily card-sessions, surely? How could he, when he had two people from his own street, for victims? She could imagine how his listeners, would lap up his revelations. They wanted their daily gossip. It did not matter who supplied them with it.

She decided to have nothing to do with Hariharan in future. But she had her doubts if that would be possible.

You are a fool, a fool, a fool. She chided herself. What's the difference between you and the other girls? They are ensnared by the spider's web and submit without protest. You are walking straight into the same trap, though you shout feminism. More's the pity!

She shook herself as if replying to the accusation.

'No, I won't be so stupid.'

She was in a listless mood when she walked to the bus stand that evening. She wanted to avoid talking to anyone and walked along, her gaze fixed straight ahead.

'Meenu! Meenu!'

Rukmini's voice.

She turned. There was a happy look today on Rukmini's face. She held a packet in her hand – much larger than the previous day's.

'Did you give that pakoda to my boy, Meenu? Did he eat it?'

Meenu stood silent for a brief while saddened by Rukmini's eagerness. How was she going to tell her?

'Mami! You stay quite close by, I think. I'm feeling rather thirsty…'

'Come along. I'd be only too glad if you came to my house, though something prevents me from inviting you myself.'

Meenu walked along with her in silence.

The house was near the bus stand. Women from the neighboring houses darted inquisitive glances in her direction. Rukmini did not look up even once. She led Meenu in.

There was a swing in the middle of the hall. The red cemented floor felt cool beneath her foot.

'Sit down. I'll bring you some water.'

Meenu felt a sudden embarrassment. How did Rukmini come to live in a house like this? It looked prosperous. Rukmini must be fairly well off now. Yet she did not look happy. With every word she spoke her eyes filled with tears.

She remembered what Rukmini had once told Lalita, 'When you don't get enough to eat, food seems the only thing that matters. But once you're full, you are disgusted with your body. I wonder if you can quite understand what I say...'

Meenu seemed to understand some of it now.

'Here's your water, Meenu. Won't you have some coffee as well?'

'No, mami. It's getting late.'

Rukmini waited for her to drink the water and then asked, 'What happened yesterday?'

Meenu looked down. 'Krishnan is a proud boy, mami!'

Rukmini went pale. 'Why, what did he say?'

'He didn't say anything. But he didn't eat what you sent him.'

At once, Rukmini's eyes filled. 'Didn't he say anything?'

'Maybe it was foolish of me to tell him it was from you!' she thought Rukmini might collapse if she told her how Krishnan had flung the pakodas away into the street. 'He just left the packet out in the porch and went in and slammed the door shut', she said.

Rukmini stood silent.

'I'm sorry mami. I ought to have given it without telling him you had sent it.'

'Nothing wrong in your telling him, Meenu. After all, how long can we go on deceiving him?'

'Mami, I hope you won't misunderstand me. You say you left that house because you found it impossible to continue there. So why don't you put it out of your mind completely? You are just torturing yourself, now, aren't you?'

Rukmini looked at her in surprise. Then she said with a sad smile, 'You are right, Meenu. It's foolish to have one foot in the river and the other on the bank. But a clean break is just not possible. Submissive people don't suffer as much as those who rebel, Meenu. As long as I lived there, in the Brahmin quarter, only my stomach seemed to be alive. But now my heart seems to be alive!'

'Let me go then, mami. It's getting late.'

'Meenu, I have a request to make. Please make Krishnan understand that I'm not as bad a woman as he imagines. Could you somehow, gradually, do that, Meenu...'

As Meenu climbed down the front steps of the house, she could hear Rukmini sobbing.

Whichever way you look at it, women get the worst deal in life.

'Submissive people don't suffer as much as those who rebel.'

How true! All protest is considered a crime, no matter how just it is.

She thought suddenly of Balu-teacher, Rukmini's husband. How was he affected by Rukmini's desertion? His ego must have been affronted. He must have been in a rage, and everyone must have sympathised with him! How well protected our menfolk are!

Meenu reached home more tired than usual. When she went in past the porch, she heard her mama bellowing: 'We've had enough! I don't want you fussing over that girl any more. Pack her off today. What does she think she's going to college for? To study, or to make love?'

CHAPTER TWENTY-THREE

The force and fury of the words stunned Meenu. She felt guilty. How was she going to tackle this problem?

'Remember how strongly you spoke for her? 'A sensible girl' you called her. Girls don't take long to take leave of their senses. I told you so.'

Her manni's reply came in a low voice. 'Somebody must have seen something. And how he goes round spreading stories. Please don't take such talk seriously.'

'Even if it's nothing but tittle-tattle, I just don't want any of it.'

'But Meenu is not likely to behave foolishly…'

'Shut up. Nobody asked for your advice. Didn't I tell you it's risky to keep a grown-up girl with us? But who listens to anything I say in this house?'

Calming herself, Meenu stepped into the hall. Pretending not to notice the rising fury on Sabhesan's face and the fear on her manni's face, she went to her room. Raju, who had been looking out of the window biting his nails, sat up with a start upon hearing her enter.

Meenu put her books on the table.

'Meenu!'

The house shook with the roar. Raju trembled slightly and Meenu noticed that there were tears in his eyes. She patted him lightly on the back and came out of her room.

'Yes, mama!'

'You needn't go to college anymore.'

'But why?'

'You don't go there to study. That's why.'

'But who told you so?'

'The whole village says so!'

'Then show them the marks I got in the half-yearly exams!'

'Be quiet! What were you doing in the library today? Tell me that.'

'I was looking for a book.'

'With whom?'

'I don't quite follow your questions, mama!'

Another wave of anger swept over Sabhesan's face. 'What was that? Don't try your tricks with me! Whom were you billing and cooing with?'

He was coming at her with his hand raised. Meenu stepped aside. If she kept quiet now, he would crush her for good.

'Mama! Please lower your voice. What has provoked you? What do you imagine has happened? Please listen to what I have to say.'

'I'm not going to listen to you!'

'How can you judge without listening to me? You ask me to stop my studies and go home, just like that. So you've got to listen to my side of the story.'

'You can make a good speech, I know. That's what comes of educating you! The whole village is talking about you now. What are you going to say about that?'

'The village is foolish, irresponsible. But you are an educated, experienced man. I find it hard to believe that you can talk so, without bothering to find out what really happened!'

His face relaxed slightly, with that little sop to his ego.

'I don't want any more details,' he said. 'What Balu said was bad enough!'

'Balu-teacher? That small minded, small-hearted man?' Meenu fumed.

'Do you expect him to be anything else when he sees a stranger holding you by the waist?'

Meenu was shaken. Who could say how much Balu had made up? How was she to extricate herself from this situation? She decided to deny everything and try to browbeat him into believing her version.

'What utter lies! Bring him here. Let me ask him a few questions. I'd like to ask him if he had left his spectacles at home. I'd like to ask him if he has started suspecting every woman in the place, just because his wife ran off. What proof has he for all that he says he saw?' She stopped, suddenly dismayed by what she had just said.

Slightly ashamed, Meenu continued: 'I am sorry. I have no right to talk about other people's affairs. But that man has told you a pack of lies. The librarian didn't come today and Lecturer Hariharan was in charge there. I went to take a book out. When I couldn't find it, he came to help me look for it. That's when Balu-teacher came in.'

'So Hariharan looked for the book with his hand round your waist!'

Meenu burst out laughing.

'Balu is quite inventive! Nobody held me by the waist or the feet! If anyone does, I'll break his leg for him!'

'I don't care about what you plan to do. Anyway, the whole street is agog with the news. You can't go to college after this.'

Meenu was astonished.

'Why should I stop going to college? Why should I behave as if I were guilty? I'm not afraid of anyone. I've done nothing wrong. You can go and ask those who let their tongues wag – what memories, what guilty memories, make them talk so. I'm not going to move an inch from here till I complete my B.A. I can't be frightened by anything that anybody might say. You can question me, if there is a complaint from my college. But don't rave against me, just because some jaundiced tattler thinks he has seen something.'

Meenu rushed back into her room.

Raju was still staring vacantly and standing where she had left him.

What next? Sabhesan seemed to have been silenced, at least for the present. If she had let herself be intimidated, she might have been packing by now.

Meenu sat down and laid her face on the table. She had managed somehow today. But how long could she continue here? Could she be sure that Hariharan wouldn't try something funny again?

'So Hariharan looked for the book with his hand round your waist!'

She felt like laughing all over again.

'Meenu akka!'

'Yes, Raju?'

'Are you going back home?'

'No, I'm not.'

'But father was angry with you, wasn't he?'

'He won't be, again!'

Raju kept looking at her, vaguely confused. Then, coming up to her he said, 'I'm going out to play.'

'By all means!' said Meenu, a little surprised, and added: 'Don't worry. I won't go anywhere, I promise.'

Her mama had fallen silent. Again, she leaned forward on the table. She would have liked to go and punch that Balu really hard! And Hariharan deserved no less! She must warn him that she'd report him to the Principal if he meddled with her again. Would she have the guts to do that?

Feeling Lalita's soft touch on her shoulders, Meenu looked up and smiled.

'What's it, manni?'

'It's for me to ask you.'

'You've heard Balu's version. You've heard mine. What more is there to hear?'

Lalita smiled. 'I'm not going to ask you anything. You're a clever girl and I know you'll be able to handle any situation.'

Meenu marvelled at the delicacy with which her manni had put it.

'You mean you don't quite believe what I said?'

'I do. But I have my doubts about Hariharan. Whether we can trust him, and if so, how far…'

Meenu looked at her, surprised. 'But manni, I'll be careful.'

'That's all I expect from you.'

Meenu resolved to be careful for her manni's sake.

Unexpectedly, Sabhesan went out, came back, ate his food and went to bed, all without uttering a single word. Nobody had ever dared to answer him as she had, thought Meenu. This was a kind of shock therapy for him…

She had nearly forgotten it all when she left for college next morning.

Hariharan was cleaning his car and watched her get into the cart. He continued polishing vigorously. That made her think of his sister, Manju. He had not spoken of her or about Helen Keller's book. Had she read it? And perhaps rid herself of her self-pity?

'My sister doesn't like my talking to any pretty girl.'

Then why did he talk to her? Only when his sister was away, did he muster the courage to tease her! He didn't even look at her the day he brought Manju to the temple, Meenu remembered.

What were those colourful phrases he had used yesterday? 'How close I feel to you! It's something I have been feeling for a long time.' And again, 'But I'll make you believe it, Meenu!'

No man was to be believed. Least of all, a man with a toothy grin.

She walked fast and entered the college without a single glance at anything round her. Climbing the stairs she heard a soft 'Meenu!' behind her.

She turned and exasperated 'Oh!' escaped her.

'You aren't fed up with me, Meenu, are you?'

'No more attention from you, please. I've had enough trouble with my mama yesterday.'

'But you handled him somehow, didn't you?'

'He can't be handled much longer. I've received an ultimatum now!'

'That Balu-teacher deserves to be tied up and beaten soundly!'

'If you'd been in his place, would you have kept mum?'

'Of course. I'm a man of some refinement.'

'Your refinement can be quite dangerous to others. I prefer Balu!'

'No more about him, please. It's enough to make one jealous! But I've got something to tell you—Manju wants to meet you.'

She looked startled. 'What?'

'Yes. She does want to meet you. She's a bit different after reading Helen Keller's book.'

She felt glad. But then, this might be just another ruse to attract her attention. She grew wary.

'I'm so glad to hear that. You can make her read more books like that. The magazines are full of stories of handicapped people – how they have managed to lead useful and happy lives. Let her read them.' She began to climb the stairs hastily. He caught her hand at once.

'Meenu, please listen to what I have to say!'

She jerked her hand free.

Controlling her anger with an effort, she said, 'Mr. Hariharan! Please leave me alone. If you are going to pester me like this, I'll leave for Madras tonight.'

'Meenu! Please, don't misunderstand me.'

'It's not enough that I don't misunderstand you. The village should not misunderstand you either. I cannot continue here if you behave as you do.'

Noticing the slight mockery in his eyes, she hastened to add: 'You see me as a mere woman. You can't imagine that I could have thoughts, goals and ideals of my own.'

Strangely, her eyes misted over.

He looked at her in surprise and said apologetically: 'Sorry, Meenu. I won't trouble you again.'

As she watched him walk away without looking back, she felt a pang of remorse.

CHAPTER TWENTY-FOUR

'How did you fare, Meenu?'

The question came from behind her, just as she was about to leave the college, after her exams. She turned to look. It was her classmate Vanaja.

'Not too bad!' replied Meenu.

'You'd have done very well, I know. You've always stood first in our class.'

'How about you, Vanaja?'

'I've done very badly. But then I didn't prepared well.'

'But why didn't you?'

'Oh, Meenu, I'm not really interested in studies. For me, college is just a stepping stone to marriage. A graduate has better prospects in the marriage market than a non-graduate, that's all.'

Meenu was astonished. 'That's odd, Vanaja. You're a woman, an individual. Not a commodity! You're not going to hang the B.A. diploma round your neck and await the bridegroom's inspection, are you?'

'Go on!' laughed Vanaja. 'I don't go analysing things! If a girl does her B.A., it adds to her glamour. That's all there is to it!'

'Isn't it foolish to study for somebody else's sake, Vanaja? We need education for ourselves. We need to think for ourselves.'

'Don't bore me with that talk, Meenu. I'm not going to work. I'm just going to be married and have children.'

'Well, of course!' laughed Meenu. 'By all means! Only, do a bit of planning!'

As Vanaja went off in search of a more interesting friend, Meenu raged silently. Such were our young people! Even a Rukmini seemed preferable to such Vanajas! That illiterate woman had somehow broken free of her shackles...

In the last three years Meenu had got to know Rukmini fairly well. Rukmini never mentioned Krishnan after he had flung away her gift. Meenu gradually grew to appreciate Rukmini's ability to think for herself. Rukmini's account of her ordeal as Balu's wife convinced Meenu that she had been right to leave him. This second man seemed to treat her well, at least as a human being, and a woman. If a man is allowed to remarry, why not a woman? Lalita manni would be shocked to hear such talk.

But her manni's ideas and philosophy of life were on another plane. There was an unbridgeable gap between her own ideas and Lalita's.

Yet the last three years had greatly increased her respect for Lalita. Each day had brought its revelation. Now Meenu knew that if her manni seemed subdued, it was not out of fear. It was only that nothing really seemed to offend her. Compassion within her forgave all. 'All the evil in this world is the result of man's ignorance. My only sorrow is for this ignorance', Lalita had said. Those words were not just high flown nonsense, Meenu realised. And she had admitted as much, 'Do you know manni, you remind me of something!'

'What's that?'

'I've often watched my mother standing before the pictures of the goddess and mumble things like 'O Ambike! O Supreme Goddess, Mother of the World!' She used to tell me that the divine mother is the personification of compassion. I understood what that meant, only after I saw you. I didn't believe in the four-armed goddess in the picture. But I do believe in you!'

'But Meenu, all women – you and I – have a spark of the Divine Mother in us. It is in our nature to show compassion. It is a pity that we forget our nature.'

Her manni was a rare woman. It was not in the nature of ordinary mortals to love everyone, including the enemy.

What a loss it was for her mama never to have perceived this. He was still the same. Flying into a rage at every trifle, abusing and beating his twelve-year old son, never stopping to think for a moment that the boy had a heart... But he had not interfered with Meenu since that day when she had told him that she was not afraid of anyone. Three whole years had since passed.

Alighting from the bus, Meenu climbed into the bullock cart awaiting her at the bus stop. She caught a glimpse of Hariharan's car as it passed the cart. She felt just a little uneasy.

Ever since that day, when Hariharan said with a crestfallen look, 'Sorry, Meenu. I won't trouble you again', he had never accosted her. Meenu was surprised he took it so seriously and, in a way, even felt disappointed. But soon she controlled herself. Any emotion is as strong or as serious as we allow it to become, she thought.

Now she could laugh at herself. How willingly do we let ourselves be entrapped by wild fancies? Thank God, she had woken up when she did. That had saved her from the village gossip-mongers and her mama's fury and from the pricks of her own conscience.

Hariharan's car had reached their street much ahead of her cart.

Raju was sitting on the porch and smiled wanly at her. She was conscious of a growing sense of unease every time she looked at him nowadays.

'Hello Raju!'

'Hello! How did you do your exams, Meenu akka?'

'Quite well. When are yours starting?'

'Next week.'

'Start preparing now, Raju!'

'Yes, I will.'

He sat still. Meenu went in, vaguely worried.

CHAPTER TWENTY-FIVE

Raju has changed a lot, thought Meenu. There was a depth in his eyes now, which had replaced the innocence of three years ago. Recently, he appeared to have withdrawn into himself like a snail. He seldom ran after the birds these days. Nor did he laugh much. He had grown quite tall and there was a shadow sprouting above his upper lip. He had no close friends. Even with her, he was no longer his old talkative self.

She went to the well at the back. The portia tree was in flower. She drew some water and splashed it on her face.

'How did you do today's paper, Meenu?'

'Quite well, manni!'

'How many days to go?'

'Another fifteen.'

'What are you going to do after that, Meenu?'

Meenu laughed. 'Pack my things and go back to Madras!'

Lalita's face fell.

'It's going to be hard for me, Meenu!'

'Remember when mama asked me to pack? I've overstayed his order by more than two years!'

'You mustn't always keep remembering such things, Meenu!'

'I'm not that sensitive. Memories don't really hurt me, manni.'

Lalita went in and brought her some coffee.

'Raju and I – we're both going to miss you terribly, Meenu!'

Meenu could think of nothing to say.

'Meenu akka, don't go away, please!' pleaded Raju.

She came out, one hand round Raju, coffee in the other.

'There's still plenty of time left for me to leave, Raju.'

'But this is your final B.A. I know, you'll leave for Madras once the exam is over, won't you?'

'I want to study further, Raju. And to do my M.A., I'll have to go to Madras. Why don't you come with me to Madras? After all I stayed here all this while for your sake. So Raju, now it's your turn.'

'But I can't!'

'Why not?'

'I can't leave this place, Meenu akka.'

'Why not?'

'I'd be scared of any new place.'

'But I'm going to be there with you.'

'No! I just can't come!'

Meenu was overcome by pity for the boy. What he said was quite true. He would collapse from sheer fright if uprooted from familiar surroundings.

'Meenu akka!...' This was a new voice calling from the front. She was surprised.

It was Krishnan. He had not shot up like Raju but his face bore the stamp of a maturity beyond his years. Glad at his unexpected visit, Meenu welcomed him.

'Come in, Krishnan. How are you?'

'Fine!'

There was a strained smile on his cheerless face. But a new light shone in his eyes. In his own way, he had changed as much as Raju.

'Sit down Krishnan. What will you have?'

'Nothing just now, akka!'

'Raju, ask mother for some tiffin and coffee for Krishnan, will you?'

Abruptly, Krishnan sat down on the pial and, burying his face between his upraised knees, began to cry.

'Why, Krishnan, what's the matter?'

He pulled himself together and wiped his eyes.

'It's all right, akka. It's good to cry when we feel like crying.'

'Why cry at all? People don't cry for nothing.'

'I think the real reasons for crying are always old reasons.'

Meenu could sense the bitterness that lay behind his precociousness, and changed the subject.

'You are two classes higher than Raju, aren't you?'

'Yes.'

'That means, the Tenth?'

'Yes.'

'Your exams must be over by now, did you do well?'

'I don't know...' Then he continued in a low voice, half-smiling, 'I've lost faith in everything – these people, their exams, their words...'

Shaken by the bitterness of the words, Meenu put a hand on his shoulder. 'Let's make another world, Krishnan! It shall be what we want it to be!'

'It can't be here on this earth. Maybe up there, in the heavens,' he smiled wryly.

Meenu looked at him in amazement. He held her hand impulsively. 'Anyway, thanks a lot, Meenu akka. Goodbye!'

He walked away without a single backward glance.

It was some time later that Meenu realised that he had not touched the tiffin or the coffee.

The next day was a holiday for Meenu. She was busy preparing for her next examination when Lakshmi came in running.

'Meenu, that boy's been missing!'

'Which boy?'

'Krishnan!'

'What? Slow down a bit. How long has he been missing?'

'Since last evening.'

That must be after he had left her!

'Seems he went off in a huff.'

'Why?'

'Don't you know, Meenu? Balu Vadyar has brought a woman home.'

What else now, wondered Meenu.

'Won't you come to the temple, Meenu akka?'

Meenu looked up from her books. Raju was begging her with his eyes.

'I've got such a lot to study, Raju. I don't think I'll have the time...'

'Do you have an exam tomorrow?'

'No. Only the day after.'

'Then you can study for it tomorrow, can't you?'

Meenu found his persistence amusing. 'What's the matter, Raju? What's the hurry to go to the temple today?'

Raju smiled shyly.

'My exams begin tomorrow.'

'So what?'

'I want God to help me.'

'If we study well, we'll do well. Where does God come in?'

Meenu sensed Raju's helplessness.

'That's quite all right with you, Meenu akka. You can study well. So you get good marks!'

'If you study really hard, you, too, can get good marks.'

There were tears in Raju's eyes. 'I just can't do well. My teacher knuckles me on the head everyday in class, saying 'Go break your head before Goddess Panaiyatha. Only she can give you marks'.

'These teachers!' thought Meenu angrily.

'Well then, let's go to the Panaiyatha temple if that's the only way you'll gain confidence. It's a nice walk for me, too. Come on.'

Lakshmi went along with them.

'I wanted to ask you to go out. You shouldn't pore over books all day long,' she said.

'But Lakshmi, it never seems enough, however much I read!'

'Why strain yourself? Anyway you will marry some fellow and start cooking!'

Meenu laughed. No use arguing with Lakshmi. She lived in a different world altogether.

'Just wait till you finish your exams. Your mother will marry you off at once.'

'But you don't expect me to agree to get married, do you?'

'You won't then?'

'No, not I. I'm going to study further!'

'And then?'

'I'm going to work. There's a lot of suffering in this world, Lakshmi. I'll try to help people in some way I can.'

Lakshmi laughed. 'Which sort of suffering do you think you can remove? As long as there are people in this world, there's bound to be suffering.'

'Why fight and argue? What have I achieved by all my arguing?' thought Meenu.

Lakshmi laughed again. 'All right. So you want to do social work. Does it mean you are not going to marry at all?'

'Perhaps I will, if I meet someone I like. Well, what about you? Why are you alone?'

'Why bother about me?'

'You discuss everybody else's affairs, but won't tell me anything about yourself. That's not fair!'

Lakshmi's face fell.

'Well my story is a story of just three sentences. I got married. I found out that he chased another woman. So I left him. That's all.'

'Why didn't you marry again? Or don't you think that people should remarry?'

'It's not that my people won't allow me to remarry, but I just don't want to marry again.'

'Are you by any chance waiting for him to return to you, as that woman Kannagi did, in the epic?'

'Not at all. I'll shoo him away if he comes back... You'd laugh if I told you any more.' Lakshmi paused for a moment. 'No Meenu, you won't understand!'

'Oh yes, I will, Lakshmi, do tell me!'

Lakshmi's face was stirred by old memories.

'They married me off to my maternal mama. I was madly in love with him long before my marriage, since I had been brought up expecting to marry him ever since I was a little girl. Now that I've left him, do you think I'll be able to love anyone else?'

Meenu walked along in silence. Lakshmi seemed to have suffered. Yet how did she manage to be so cheerful?

'It's only because of women like you that these men are so abominably arrogant!' said Meenu.

'You can't crush them. Try what you may! But Meenu, there is still something called love, don't you think so?'

'No, I don't!'

'No use arguing with you then!'

As they passed Balu Vadyar's house, painful memories of Krishnan stirred in Meenu. She remembered how he used never to leave that house, ever since his mother had left them. How did he suddenly leave it? She remembered his face with its beatific smile. There had been no news of him yet...

The house was locked from within. Balu must be in there with his new woman. Lakshmi said that the woman had not been seen outside at all. How long will this shyness last? A few more days... and she will be seen sitting on the porch... perhaps Balu also... What right had this man to slander Meenu? Or even his wife Rukmini?

Raju was silent even after they had left the street and entered the fields. He was staring blankly at the storks bobbing up and down. Surprised at his silence, Meenu said, 'Look! The storks, Raju! See them?'

'Yes.'

'Let's run, shall we?'

'No, akka!'

'Why Raju? Why not?'

'Somehow. I don't feel like it today.'

'Don't be so scared of the exams, Raju!'

Raju walked on in silence, looking up at the sky. He was more scared of his father than his exams, and nothing that she might say was likely to soothe him, she thought.

He stood for a long time before the deity, his eyes closed in prayer.

'So the exams are here! Pray hard, boy, pray hard!' said the priest.

Raju did not smile sheepishly as before. He began to walk round the shrine, ignoring the man.

'The boy's grown up!' he said.

Meenu came out hurriedly, not wishing to waste any time. Then she stopped, surprised. She saw Hariharan pushing Manju in her wheel-chair. The unexpected encounter inundated her with a sudden flood of emotion that surprised and embarrassed her. She watched Hariharan's face brightening. 'Hello!' she said, including both of them in her smile.

'Hello!'

To her surprise, Manju was smiling at her too.

'So you are still in this village, are you?' asked Hariharan.

'And still studying in the college where you teach!'

'Enough of your banter!' said Manju. Then she gave Meenu a long look.

'Why don't you ever come to visit us, Meenu?' she asked.

Meenu looked at her, wide-eyed with surprise. Had Manju forgotten how she had shouted 'Get out!' to her that day?

'Is it because I shouted at you that day?'

'Oh, no. I'm not one to mind things that much!'

'Then what has kept you away?'

After darting a glance at Hariharan, Meenu looked again at Manju.

'If it had been Madras, I'd have come everyday. But in this place I have to be careful. Anyway, you seemed to find my visit painful. So why make matters worse?'

Manju seized her hands in an impulsive gesture. 'I'm sorry about that. Please do come, Meenu!'

'Yes, I will. After the exams.'

'O God! Fifteen days to go!' The eagerness in Hariharan's voice sent a thrill of joy through Meenu.

What was happening to her, she wondered.

'I think you have four days free after your next paper. You can come one of those days, can't you?' said Hariharan.

He seemed to be fully briefed on her time-table. She felt like laughing.

'Are you still afraid of the village?' he asked.

'Not at all. I'll come the day after, in the evening. I don't have to live in fear of this village any longer. I'm going back to Madras once my exams are over.'

Meenu found it hard to concentrate on her studies for the rest of the day. How foolish, how utterly foolish of her to be distracted by a single meeting with him, she thought ruefully.

CHAPTER TWENTY-SIX

It was on the evening of the second day. She had finished the day's exam, come home, had her tiffin and coffee and gone directly to Hariharan's house. Hariharan opened the door, gave a perfunctory smile and said 'I'm honoured!'

Presently he left, with 'Have a chat with Manju. I've got to go out.' Again she wondered why she felt cheated.

Manju was shaking with violent sobs. For a moment Meenu stood looking at her, at a loss for words.

Had Manju really changed from the girl who had ordered her out of the house to the one who had asked her why she no longer came to her house?

But what could have happened to upset her in those past two days. She called, 'Manju!' Manju wiped her tears and looked up. 'Oh, come on in! I was afraid you wouldn't turn up!'

Meenu smiled. 'Afraid?'

'I was really worried. I don't get the chance to meet people as you do.'

'Are you really the same Manju who would not talk to any one?'

Manju leant back on her chair and closed her eyes. The sight of the tears flowing from her closed eyes made Meenu regret her words. 'Sorry Manju!' she said.

Manju recovered herself.

'You were quite right. I was very foolish. I used to be so eaten up with jealousy and anger. Why had God picked me alone to be so helpless, dependant on others for everything, while the rest of the world went walking, running and jumping? I used to get furious with my mother, blame her for my polio, accuse her of neglect.'

Suddenly she looked at Meenu and smiled. 'But I know better now. Maybe we get only what we are destined to get. Anyway, it is foolish to blame anyone for our misfortunes. Wisdom lies in getting on with life in spite of everything.'

Meenu sat smiling at her.

'Thanks to you, Meenu, I've changed.'

'Oh, no! After all, I've spoken to you only once before now.'

'Remember what you told me that day? That to be mentally retarded or to be blind is greater afflictions than to have useless legs? I raged for a long time after you left me. I shouted at everybody. But my brother was my main target.

I thought he must have invited you purposely to insult me. But right through that madness, your words came back to me and made me think. Then came that book!'

Meenu let her talk.

'My brother had brought me books of that sort before; but I had thrown every one of them away. He left Helen Keller's autobiography on the table. Luckily, it caught my eye when I was in a good mood and I began to read it. As I went on, I was amazed. What an extraordinary woman! Have you read it, Meenu?'

'Yes.'

'What a terrible fate? To lose her eyesight and also her speech—and the way she struggled to overcome her fate! What she achieved was a miracle, Meenu! A thrill went through me when I closed the book! I realised then how I had wasted my life, not using any of my abilities or the facilities I had been blessed with.

Manju continued, gazing at the rafters and as if talking to herself. 'For about a week after that I didn't talk to anyone. I was deep in thought all that time. I began doing things myself whenever I could without expecting my other to do them for me. Perhaps mother herself made me so helpless by never allowing me to do anything for myself.'

She turned to look at Meenu and smiled brightly. 'But I'm not out to blame anyone. There must be a reason for everybody's behavior—a reason however tucked away. Thank God, I'm out of the dark into broad daylight now—all because of a little book. Can you believe that, Meenu?'

Meenu said, 'I'm so glad Manju!'

'I must thank you for everything, Meenu!'

'Why, what did I do for you?'

'I know it was you who sent that book.'

Meenu just smiled.

'I would not have succeeded without my brother's help. I can never forget all that he has done for me. He has had no thought for himself for the past two or three years.'

Then why was she crying today?

'He taught me typing and shorthand and made me read a lot. My mind is broader now; it's as if I had traveled. Earlier, I gave up doing any of the exercises that the doctor prescribed. I've started doing them again. Brother brought me some aids from Madras that I can use by myself. I can now walk for a few minutes, holding on to the wall, Meenu!'

'Oh, I'm so happy!'

'I shall never forget that it's all because of my brother and you, Meenu.'

'Who made you change is not all that important. The fact is that you have changed.'

But Manju didn't seem to have heard her.

'I've begun to feel I shouldn't be a burden to anyone.'

Meenu looked at her in some confusion. 'But Manju, your family will never think of you as a burden!'

'Whether they do or not, I'm nothing but a burden!' She was tearful again.

'Why, Manju, I thought you'd changed and were full of a new confidence. But here you go shedding tears all over again! Now that you can look after yourself, why ever should you feel you're a burden to others?'

'I'm imposing myself on them by staying at home.'

'Stupid!'

'Oh, no. I've thought about it.'

'Well, suppose you were a burden, what are you going to do about it?'

'I've got to leave the house!'

'Goodness! And then?'

'I'll join one of the homes meant for people like me. I can learn some craft there and earn a living. Seeing other handicapped people can toughen me, and broaden my outlook.'

It was not a bad idea, Meenu thought.

'I really can say nothing, Manju. It is for your people to decide. Perhaps you can do something from home and earn. Anyway, you can boost your self-confidence even here.'

'That's just a temporary solution. Actually it's best for me and the others if I leave home.'

'How can you say so? Your father, mother, and brother all dote on you!'

'That's what's keeping them all in shackles!'

'I don't quite see what you are driving at.'

'As long as I am here, my brother can't marry!'

'Oh, I see.'

'And he won't marry!'

'But that's for him to decide, is it not?'

'He doesn't think he has any choice in this matter!' Manju's face took an angry look.

'Don't let your imagination run away with you.'

'I'm not imagining things. I know he wants to get married but won't because of me.'

She went on. 'He has done so much for me, Meenu! I want him to live a normal life and get married like everyone else.'

'There's nothing wrong in that, certainly.'

'But he doesn't understand. He fought with me over this even today. He threatened to leave the house if I pressed him. The thought that I'm ruining other's lives is hell to me. Nobody seems to understand.'

Hariharan apparently had unsuspected depths.

Meenu stood up. 'Everything will happen in its own good time. I may not be wiser to hustle him.'

'He's too deep for me. Only you can make him change his mind.'

'Me?'

'Manju!' That was Hariharan's resonant voice from behind. Meenu turned to look at him.

'Manju! How often have I told you to put this idea out of your head! What made you tell Meenu all this? Meenu, you'd better go now. Your exams are not over yet. Don't add our problems to yours.'

Surprised at the tone of his voice, Meenu left.

'Goodbye, Manju! Keep smiling!'

He's too deep for me. Only you can make him change his mind. Manju heard this over and over again.

But why should I? Then she laughed at herself. What did she have to do with these two people? Two more weeks, and she'd be gone. Time to shake the dust of this place off her feet.

Time to forget this village and its people. Interesting people, though. They must be the same in every village.

Pathetic creatures with not the least idea of how pathetic they were. If one could say to them, 'Arise! Take up your bed and walk.' In Lalita manni's phraesology, they were immersed in ignorance.

As she was climbing the front steps of her house, Meenu heard her mama.

'It's all my previous karma! Why were you born my son? Wish you had not been born! Such simple sums! You can't do these, you thickheaded fool'

'Oh! Please don't! Don't hit him!' cried Lalita.

'Get away from here, you woman!'

Meenu ran in.

CHAPTER TWENTY-SEVEN

Sabhesan kept hitting Raju madly, this way and that, but Raju was not crying. There was no fear in his eyes. He stood silent, as if bearing a cross. She leapt between the two, covering Raju.

'Oh don't hit him, mama! Please don't!'

Sabhesan glowered at her but lowered his lifted hand.

'Do you know how he's done his maths paper? Every single sum's wrong. What am I to do with this idiot?'

'Is there any rule that says only maths wizards have a right to life in this world?'

'Anyone can live like a sheep or a cow! Better die than live like cattle!'

'O Lord! What words are these?' cried Lalita.

'Look at this son you've begotten! Go and ask your Lord yourself!'

Sabhesan flung a towel over his shoulder and walked out.

Raju was now sitting on the floor, his hands round his bent knees, his eyes staring ahead. His cheeks and back bore the red weals of his recent beating. It would be better if he cried now, thought Meenu.

Lalita stood facing the window, looking out, tears streaming down her cheeks.

Meenu sat near Raju on the floor and laid a hand on his back softly. Raju shivered slightly as if the touch had suddenly brought him back to consciousness.

'What happened today, Raju?'

He said, 'What had to happen, has happened!'

'You mean you did the sums wrong!'

Now he turned to look at her with a sad smile. 'I haven't done them correctly, have I?'

'It's not a crime to do sums wrong, Raju!'

Raju said, 'Of course it is! Didn't you hear all that my father said?'

He always says things like that when he's angry. Don't take it too hard!'

'How would you take it, Meenu akka, if you were me?'

'I can't say Raju. All the same, you shouldn't mind too much.'

Lalita came to him, wiping away her tears. 'Look, Raju! It doesn't matter if you haven't done this paper well. We need not all be geniuses at mathematics. It is much more important for us to be good and kind. You must look after our lands and be just to everyone. That's all I want of you, Raju! I don't want you to appear for the I.A.S.'

Raju sat staring as if he had heard nothing. Suddenly he laughed. 'I won't be born again as a human being, Meenu akka. As a stork, or a butterfly, maybe! Then you'll have a chance to fly away and escape from anyone who comes to hit you!'

'Don't talk so, Raju', said Lalita. Father is really very fond of you. Only he doesn't know how to show it.'

But Raju went on. 'And supposing that I can't be born a stork, I'll stay back in heaven. I won't be born here again.'

'What silly talk, Raju!'

'Going to the temple is a sheer waste of time, akka. God is not there. He is not anywhere at all. That's why he doesn't listen to my prayers.'

'Do have faith in Him, my darling! He certainly cares for you!' said Lalita tearfully.

'Lies! Nothing but lies! Things wouldn't be like this if there were a God. Saroji Mami wouldn't have died. Krishnan wouldn't have left home! Manju akka wouldn't have lost her legs! I wouldn't be an idiot!'

'You're not an idiot, Raju! You'll understand these things when you grow older. You're making me sad, Raju. Don't talk so bitterly!'

'Don't worship Him anymore, amma. And don't ask me to recite those hymns. God can't hear any of that. He's not there at all. He's only up in the skies.'

'Get up Raju!' Meenu said sharply. She was troubled by his delirious words. 'This is not the time to discuss God's existence and whereabouts. Come on! You've got to study for tomorrow!'

'Yes! I'll study, I'll study. I'll study.'

'Raju! Get up!'

Raju walked as if in a dream and went into the inner room.

Lalita said in a barely audible voice, 'Only God can save the boy!'

'Manni, I too would like to know if your God is really there!'

'Meenu! Don't! I'm sick with dread, Meenu.'

'Sorry, sorry, manni.'

She took Raju along to their room to study.

Every time Meenu turned to look at Raju, she found him gazing vacantly ahead. She kept reminding him to study.

Sabhesan did not speak to anyone for the rest of the day.

The next morning, when Raju was getting ready to leave for his examination, Meenu heard Lalita tell him, 'Say your prayers, Raju. Do a namaskaram.'

'No. I'm not going to!'

'The holy ash?'

'No. I don't want any of it!'

Was this the same Raju who used to pray so fervently for intelligence, eyes closed, hands touching his ears, and all that? Meenu wondered. Someone came and stood behind her chair. She turned and found Raju.

'What's it, Raju?' she asked. 'Going to write your exam? Good luck!'

He held her by the shoulder briefly. 'Thank you very much, Meenu akka!'

'Don't lose heart, Raju! Be a brave boy!' she said hastily, noticing his eyes moistening.

Wiping his eyes with the back if his hand, Raju smiled faintly at her. 'Okay!'

For a long time after he had gone, Meenu remembered the wan smile and those tear-clouded eyes. She wondered if Lalita had had anything to eat since last night. But she brushed aside all worries and tried to concentrate on her next exam. She needed a book from the library and left for college soon after lunch, afraid that she would be distracted and troubled if she stayed at home.

'I'll spend some time in the library and be back in the evening, manni.'

'All right, dear.'

Once she sank into the chair in the library with a book in hand, she was lost to the world till the librarian reminded her that it was closing time.

There was an unusual rush at the bus stop today. If she missed the bus now, she'd have to wait for at least half an hour for the next one. Still, she would not be able to get in, she retreated.

'Meenu!'

She turned and saw Rukmini. 'Here comes someone to add her share to the day's sorrow!' thought Meenu gloomily. She had not met Rukmini after Krishnan's disappearance.

'How are you, Mami?'

'Fine, as ever! Your exams seem to be going on.'

'Yes. Come, let's stand a bit farther away.'

Rukmini avoided looking at Meenu.

'Mami, you must've heard Krishnan has run away.'

'Yes, I heard. Any further news?'

'No.'

'Have the police been informed?'

'So they say.'

'These are confused times, Meenu. Somehow the young are the hardest hit.'

Meenu thought of Raju.

'Because grown-ups forget that youngsters can think!'

Rukmini hung her head.

'You would have done the same thing, Meenu if you had been in my place.'

'I'm not blaming you, mami!'

'That man seems to have brought a woman home to live with him now. Nothing at home to eat. But he needs a woman!'

Rukmini looked angry. How she must hate that Balu Vadyar, thought Meenu. But most to be pitied now was Krishnan, the product of their union...

'Who knows where my child is now! He'll fare well if that's his fate. Anyway, if he had stayed on there, that man would have ruined him.'

The bus arrived. As Meenu was about to board it, she noticed that Rukmini was pregnant. It was just as well that Krishnan had left home...Krishnan, the boy with a sense of responsibility...who had shaken himself free of everything. He had said, 'I've lost faith in everything. These people, their exams, their words...'

He'll manage to get along, somehow. If only he could learn to laugh again...

Meenu had begun to feel close to the people of this village. Closer than she had ever felt to the people of Madras. Could she ever be at home again in Madras? Forget these green fields and the storks?

The storks...And Raju. Dear Raju.

Why had he spoken so in the morning? As soon as she stepped out of the bus, she started walking home, without waiting for the cart. As she entered their street, a wave of panic hit her.

There was a crowd – a silent crowd gathered at Sabhesan's house. Meenu ran past them and went in.

Raju's body lay on the floor of the central hall.

CHAPTER TWENTY-EIGHT

Meenu stood staring. Every fibre of her body cried out—Raju! Was this why?

Was this why he had come into her room with tear-laden eyes and said, 'Thank you very much, Meenu akka.'

'Raju!'

Unable to control herself any longer, she dashed across to the body and seizing the face, now leaden and lifeless, began to shake it in a frenzy.

'Raju, look at me! Call me Meenu akka, Raju! Why did you do this? Why, why?'

The tears flowed now, unheeded.

The sky.

Yes, that's where Raju had gone.

'If only we can go to the skies! It will be so lovely up there! Don't you think so, Meenu akka?'

As she covered her face and sobbed, Meenu felt folded into a tender embrace. It was Lalita, who was shaking with her own sobs.

How was she going to bear this loss?

'Meenu, don't cry Meenu! I can't bear it if you cry so, Meenu!'

The words came caressing, soft.

For the first time Meenu saw Lalita as an ordinary woman.

'What happened, manni?'

'After leaving for school from here, he seems to have gone straight to the tank and drowned himself.'

So, he had worked everything out.

Better die than live like cattle!... had been Sabhesan's words.

Hot with anger, Meenu looked round.

Sabhesan was sitting by the wall, his head in his hands. She went and stood before him.

'So now, are you satisfied?'

He bent further.

'Why do you hang your head now? Aren't you satisfied yet?'

He began to hit himself on his head.

But Meenu was too furious to stop. 'Aren't you pleased to see him lying flat there? You must be! Aren't you?'

'Stop it, Meenu!'

'Don't stop me, manni. He must realise what he has done. He never treated Raju like a child. This man's cruelty has driven the boy to his death!'

'Meenu, don't say things like that. Raju was his son too.'

'Let me have my say! Who else will dare to ask him if I don't? Did he ever behave like a father? He said it would be better to die than to live like cattle. He asked Raju why he was ever born his son.'

With streaming eyes and a heaving heart Lalita came near her. 'Meenu! Stop now.'

'No! I won't! This is murder! This man has committed a murder!'

Lalita slapped her hard on the cheeks. In a moment, Meenu controlled herself.

Lalita was standing before her, livid with rage. Only then did it dawn on Meenu that the hall was full of people. Indeed, the whole street was here.

'Sorry, manni.' She said and rushed to her room.

She could hear a loud slap from the hall – Sabhesan beating himself.

Meenu saw Raju everywhere. And heard him call her 'Meenu akka!'

How lovely these storks are, akka! Such pure whiteness!

Your heart was no less pure, Raju! We have murdered a child. How many murders of this kind do we commit everyday? Routine massacres of the innocents?

At this rate, this house is never going to prosper. Never!

Her mama did not know the power of words. He could not have understood the words uttered with such concentrated hatred could be charged with the power of the demons.

Meenu recalled what her grandmother used to say: 'Never utter a curse or a word of ill-omen. There are evil spirits always hovering in the air, just waiting to add their 'tathaasthu'—their 'Amen!' or 'May it be so!' to our negative wishes. That's how curses are fulfilled!'

Meenu had often laughed at her grandmother's admonitions. 'Tell me I shouldn't harbor negative thoughts ever, and I'll gladly listen to you granny! No need at all for your spirits – goblins stuff.' Perhaps her granny had been right, after all.

Her grandmother was Sabhesan mama's mother. Yet he had been so eloquent with maledictions. Those spirits must have added their 'thathaasthu' to his curses!

'Please stay with us here, Meenu akka! Please, won't you?'

Meenu turned sharply.

No. There was no one there.

There's nothing to keep me back here now, thought Meenu. I stayed for your sake, Raju, because I couldn't bear to see you suffer. But I could do nothing, nothing at all for you. If only I had spent more time with him this morning…'Don't lose heart, Raju. Be a brave boy!' was all I said. O God! Did he mistake that for a signal from me?

'You'll leave for Madras once your exams are over, I know.' He had said.

He must have been eating his heart out imagining her departure. The prospect of being left alone must have been terrifying. If I had only thought of all that, I would have stayed back, Raju!

The hall was full. Everyone undertook to do something. The priest who had given Raju a sarcastic blessing was there, aloof with bowed head. Hariharan's parents, who seldom stepped out of their house, were also there. And Hariharan was there, too, heavy with sorrow. There was pity in every face.

The village official had managed as usual to keep the police out of the picture.

Lalita sat in a corner, silent tears streaming down her face. Each time somebody spoke a few words of condolence to Sabhesan, he struck himself with heavy blows on the head.

By night everything was over. The whole house was washed as if Raju's memory had to be washed out of it. Meenu did not speak. Sabhesan still sat in the hall, as if nailed to the place. Lalita lay curled up in an inner room.

Lalita too must have felt enraged at the sight of the body. 'Who knew, if not she, how Sabhesan had driven the child to his death?' thought Meenu.

If she had not felt like that for at least a single, fleeting moment, she couldn't be human. To be like the drops of water on a lotus leaf after such a shock was certainly not humanly possible…

Perhaps she had always had a foreboding that such sorrow was in store for her. She must have disciplined herself, to absorb every kind of shock and remain unperturbed.

Meenu fell asleep at last.

She had three more papers before her. Shutting everything else out of her mind, impervious to all that was happening around her, she went to college and wrote her exams.

Her mother arrived from Madras. Her frequent lamentations were oddly in contrast to Lalita's subdued grief.

Her mother had planned to stay on for some time and try to console her brother and sister-in-law.

The day Meenu finished her last examination, she felt exhausted. She must go for a walk, by herself, alone. 'I'm going for a walk!' she announced.

'Take Lakshmi with you!'

'No. I don't need her!'

As she stepped out, she could hear her mother complaining to Lalita: 'Meenu hasn't changed a bit! She's always had her own way! Nobody can question her.'

'But Bala, why should she change? She knows she's doing the right thing!'

Meenu was moved by Lalita's words. This, then was her manni's compassion. A forgiveness that embraced all wrong-doers.

Meenu went past all the houses of the bleak street that was in mourning for Raju and Krishnan. Even Ganesa Padayachi's children played silently on the street. Saroji's children sat glumly on the porch of Sankaralinga Iyer's house. What a hard world it was for these children! They can't be expected to live like drops of water on a lotus leaf. They can't absorb the shocks of living. They can only run away from home or drown themselves in the tank or sit staring at the sky with lusterless eyes.

Leaving the street behind, Meenu walked along the fields. A flight of storks darted up – dazzling white above the green fields.

She thought she would not be able to walk any further. With faltering steps she reached a rock a few feet away from the path, sat down and burst into tears.

'Meenu!'

She looked up, startled.

It was Hariharan.

'Meenu! How long have I waited to see you and talk to you!'

All her restraint left her at the sight of him. It was as if she had met someone very close to her. She broke into sobs.

CHAPTER TWENTY-NINE

'Don't cry, Meenu!' said Hariharan softly. Gradually she grew quiet.

'I was so shocked, Meenu. I can quite understand what it must have been like for you. I know how you loved him!'

'I still can't believe he's dead,' she said slowly. I can still hear him call me...

'I was shocked that day when you raved at your mama. It was only later that I came to know about his temper. I wonder how you put up with him all the time.'

'Don't you wonder how that child bore the brunt of his temper for so long? Poor hapless boy! He bore it all silently. In his place, I would have fought back to show that I had some rights too!'

Hariharan smiled. 'Yes, you're good at that sort of thing.'

But Meenu went on. 'Raju was a bit weak in the head, but there was nothing really wrong with him. My mama tormented him because he was not smart. I shudder to think how he would have treated a mentally-retarded or crippled child. He had no pity for the poor boy. The mere sight of Raju brought out the worst in him. He must have felt that he himself had failed, that he himself had been defeated.'

'That, too, is a kind of crippling, Meenu. It's the crippling of the mind – more terrible than a crippled body.'

'You've put it well. It dried up his heart…'

Hariharan fell silent. After looking at her thoughtfully for some time, he asked, 'How have you done in your exams, Meenu?'

'Fairly well. I don't know how I managed to get through them in the midst of all this.'

'The Principal says you'll stand first in the University.'

'Not a chance! I'll pass, that's all!'

It was quite like old times. They were still friends, after all. They could talk.

'What are you going to do now?'

'I'm going to Madras to do my M.A.'

'And after your M.A?'

She laughed.

'I don't know. There are lots of things I want to do. Lots of dreams.'

He smiled. 'What sort of dreams?'

She spoke with some hesitation. 'I feel I must do something for our women. The plight of village children also disturbs me. We have condemned them to darkness. Something has to be done, Hariharan!'

'It is the adults who are floundering in darkness here!'

'Nothing can be done for them. They'll have to find their own way out. But I'm worried about the children...and the kind of world they are going to inherit.'

She paused. He was looking at her with interest. There was no mockery in his eyes, no playfulness. Only a sense of pride. As if there had been an unexpectedly agreeable revelation.

'What do you intend doing about it?'

'I should like to start a school in a village. If we can help ten children to grow up with healthy minds, we can make ten happy families...'

'A good project.' Suddenly he laughed.

'But you are not the only one to have dreams. Do you know, Meenu, I have a few of my own?'

'May I ask you what they are?'

'You may. I'm going to start a hospital, a sort of home for the crippled.'

Meenu clapped her hands enthusiastically.

'Good! Very good! Is that for Manju?'

He nodded. 'And for others like Manju.'

'But a scheme like that costs a lot!'

'I'm going to raise the money. I'll go to the government for help. And I'll sell some of my lands.'

'Where do you plan to set it up?'

'Here, in this village. That way, I can be with Manju. I don't like the idea of sending her away to an institution.'

Meenu thought of Manju's tears the day she had gone to meet her. 'Manju wants you to lead a normal life, Hariharan.'

'It's not enough if she alone wants it.'

'Then you might as well want it too!'

'Nor is it enough that I alone want it.'

Meenu stood up. 'It's getting late. I'd better go now.'

He moved to bar her way.

'Why don't you ask me who else should want it?'

'Because I don't want to know.'

'Let me tell you something Meenu. It's best for a dreamer to marry a dreamer. The bullocks drawing a cart need to be matched properly, as they say.'

'You'd better start looking for such a partner then!'

'Meenu! You know perfectly well what I mean.'

'It's funny, Hariharan. At times you don't care even to look at me. At other times you say such silly things!'

He laughed. 'I promised you something that day, some three years ago, remember? I've kept my promise, not even turning to look at you. You perhaps wonder why I behaved so distantly with you the day you came to see Manju. She's just started to change. I want her to change completely. I was afraid she might sulk again if I spoke to you.'

'It's late, Hariharan. I must go.'

'You haven't given me your answer yet!'

'Sorry. I'm not interested in this partnership.'

She walked and he walked by her side.

'Meenu, three years is a long time. It helped me to find out how deep my interest in you went. The more I found Manju changing, the more I admired you. It's because of you that she has changed.'

'I don't think admiration should necessarily lead to marriage. Let's be friends!'

'But Meenu, I want your love for life!'

'Hariharan, please don't press me. I have no faith in marriage. When I look at the goings-on in these families around me, I feel that marriage is a farce. It will turn me into somebody else's chattel. My dreams would become meaningless then.'

'I'll prove to you that it's not so, you are imagining things.'

'You mean, your proof will follow marriage? Sorry. I can't take that risk!'

Hariharan looked almost angry.

'Hariharan! Please try to understand me. My mind is in a whirl now. The things that have happened in this village have been so shocking, I've lost all faith in people.'

'But Meenu, there's bound to be suffering wherever people are. Cities have their own brand of hardship. It is only that in a city we don't have the time to find out about other people's problems.'

'If I increase and multiply my own problems, I won't have any time to devote to other's problems. That's what I am trying to say.' More softly she added: 'Why is it that those who join a matham or a convent are forbidden to marry? Isn't it because those who get entangled in such relationships cannot give of their best to social service?'

He walked on thoughtfully, till they reached the village street. Then he smiled at her. 'Okay, Meenu! I won't force you. If you ever happen to change your mind, let me know. I am not going to change my mind, ever.'

He took her hand in both of his and after a gentle squeeze, released it. Then he walked away.

Hariharan had changed, thought Meenu. He had gained a new depth. He was more mature.

'I am not going to change my mind, ever,' he said. Was his love that deep?

Love! Huh!

She had to admit she felt attracted to him. His looks, his smile, everything about him triggered an instant surge in her. She felt even a silly craving for his touch. This he called 'love'.

No. This was nothing but sexual attraction. Something physical, purely biological, Meenu thought. If I give in to it, I'll be lost – that'll be the end of all my dreams and ideals. She entered the Brahmin quarters.

Gopu and Venkittu were sitting on the porch of Sankaralinga Iyer's house. The woman who had replaced Saroji, was there too.

Meenu stopped for a moment. 'Are your exams over, Gopu?'

'Oh, yes!'

'What exams! The two of them never study for any exam,' said the woman.

The boys looked straight ahead as if what was said was none of their business.

'The school is no good. The teachers are no good. And the students are no good either,' declared the woman.

Saroji had hanged herself. But that did not seem to have affected the living in any way. It had made no difference to her husband's drinking and gambling. What break could these children hope for? Perhaps this woman too would leave them and run away...

No point in worrying about these people any more...She walked home looking straight ahead.

The house was silent. She remembered that her mother had probably gone to the market. Lalita's singing came to her from the back of the house.

'Varai nenche unran dunmargam...

O my mind! My restless mind!

Come, give up your evil ways.

A thousand times have I pleaded with you,

All to no avail.

But wait! I shall win yet,

And subdue you,

By that grace divine.

Meenu went in. As she crossed the front room, Lalita turned to see who it was.

'Come Meenu!' she said, with a smile. Her old smile. And that luminous aura. Meenu felt shaken.

CHAPTER THIRTY

Lalita was saddened to see that Meenu approached her with a new hesitancy.

How sad and dark she had become in the last few days, thought Lalita. Nevertheless she managed to smile.

'Come, Meenu!'

Meenu sat down by her side.

'What are you doing, manni?'

'I just felt like singing. There are times, when I am absolutely alone, when I feel I can see my mind standing before me! Then I carry on a dialogue, or a question-answer session with it. Luckily, my father taught me enough verses to tackle this problem.'

Meenu suddenly bent forward and, burying her face in Lalita's lap, began to cry. Lalita stroked her face in silence.

Let her cry. Let her sorrow be drained away. Let her not grieve alone.

'Manni...I'm sorry...'

'What about?'

'Everything. About what I did that day.'

'You were nearly out of your mind with shock, Meenu. It was your love for Raju that made you speak as you did.'

'I just couldn't bear it, manni.'

'I can understand that, Meenu. But, no matter what the provocation, we must never lose control. That's why I slapped you. It is I who should say sorry.'

'I think I'd have gone mad that day, if you hadn't slapped me. But tell me, didn't you feel as angry as I did? Tell the truth. Didn't you?'

'No...' 'I can't believe that!'

Lalita laughed mirthlessly.

'That's the trouble with you. You think anger is the only natural reaction.'

'But don't you see, my anger was justified!'

'If you turn on your mama as you did, it only means that you are making the same mistake as he did.'

'I don't follow.'

'You said he never realised that Raju had a heart. Well, did you ever stop to think he himself might have a heart?'

'I wanted to make some impression on whatever sort of heart he has. That's why I said those things!'

'He, too, wanted to impress things on Raju, and he did it in the only way he knew. But if he had known this was going to destroy his son, do you think he would have behaved as he did?'

'He certainly ought to have known!'

Lalita ran her fingers through Meenu's hair. 'There are people whose minds never grow, never broaden. Your mama is such a one and he is as worthy of pity as Raju.'

Lalita continued, 'You accused your mama of murder. Did you stop to think how it might affect him? No. Normally, you would have chosen your words carefully. You would have been just. What made you forget yourself that day? Anger! It was the same anger that had him in grip throughout. We may manage to conceal it with our refined manners. But there are people who are without refinement...'

'Did mama say anything about...all this?'

'Nothing at all...The evening...Your mama was at his evening worship. It was quite late and Raju had not returned...I panicked. I sent Lakshmi and Pavadai to look for him, and waited in the porch. Then I saw them coming. Four people along with Pavadai. Pavadai had Raju's body flung across his shoulders. I froze where I stood. Not a single word could I say. But your mama came to look, puja bowl and spoon still in hand, as if he had been called. His eyes seemed to bulge at the sight of Pavadai with Raju slung over his shoulder. The vessel dropped from his hand. He screamed, 'Oh! What have I done! The monstrous sinner that I am!' Snatching Raju's body he carried it to the hall, laid it on the floor and began to shake it crying, 'What have you done, oh what...' He began to hit himself on the head and kept raving, 'Sinner that I am! Monstrous sinner that I am!' I was more shocked than even when I first saw Raju's body.'

Meenu did not move, could not, indeed, speak.

'His heart is not a rock, Meenu. It's weaker than ours. We have accepted Raju's loss. He has not been able to come to terms with it. He's utterly broken. He hasn't spoken a word to anyone since then.'

Lalita and Meenu sat together in silence for a long time. When Bala returned from the market, Lalita got up to sort out the things she had brought with her.

'Why do you bother?' asked Bala. 'I can take care of these things. Let me do what I can as long as I'm here!'

'But how can I just sit here doing nothing?'

'I'm asking you to sit down and rest. Why can't you? What have you got to show for all your work? I'm going to be here for a mere ten days. Let me do something. Even if it won't compare with what you do, just let me do something.'

Lalita smiled to herself. What a contrast between the bustling Bala and her daughter!

'But Bala, my mind keeps going back again and again to all that happened if I sat idle.'

'All right then, if it makes things easier for you...'

Bala emptied the bag of vegetables on the floor.

After the green vegetables, came the tubers of cheppan-kizhangu tumbling down, big and small. Raju's favorite vegetable.

'Can I have some more of it, amma?'

The eager question...followed by the hesitant look...Lalita's eyes filled.

'Why, what's the matter?' enquired Bala.

'Oh, nothing, Bala.'

'What! cheppan-kizhangu?' cried Meenu. 'Please don't make any curry with it. I'm not going to eat it.'

'What's happened to you? You used to like it so!'

'Yes. Raju was fond of it...'

'Oh!'

Lalita collected all the tubers into a paper bag.

'It's all right, Bala. Just ask Lakshmi to take this to Sankaralinga Iyer's house.'

Lalita went about her other chores. It had been easy to dispose of the vegetables. But there were so many other memories. How do you get rid of the many pictures imprinted on your memory? Raju seemed to be having a bath at the well. Or sitting on the front pial. Or standing at the doorstep. Or telling her, 'If only we can go to the skies! It must be so lovely up there!'

She came into the open courtyard and looked up at the sky.

Are you happy there, Raju, with no sums to frighten you, no tables to worry you...?

'I won't be born again as a human being!'

Your stay with us must have been the leftover of a previous account in the scheme of births and rebirths...It was over and you left us. May your soul now rest in God! May you not be born again! As she thought about Raju, his death began to appear inevitable. He would have suffered if he had lived any longer.

'It's all my previous karma...Why were you born my son? It's not for us to ask such question. Reasons beyond all reason...mysteries beyond our reach...

Rukmini had come to see her two days ago. She had come through the backdoor as before, and had sat on the same platform and said in a tearful voice: 'What a cruel blow, Lalita! This should not have happened to you. God is unjust.'

'What is so special about me, mami?'

'Oh, you are like a perennial river. The rest of us are foul drains, sewers...'

'But no one is special, or exempt. All of us have to atone for what we did in our previous births, our karma...'

'It must be your karma. How else can you explain all that you have had to suffer?'

Rukmini seemed to be pregnant. Lalita felt sorry for her.

'Today's children are intelligent, Lalita. They are not what we think they are. They are capable of thinking. Just take Krishnan and what he did...No sign of him...' Tears streamed down Rukmini's face.

'No, don't cry please! Krishnan is a clever boy. He's sure to make good, somewhere...'

'That's what I tell myself...'

Sabhesan had sunk into a pathetic state. He had not spoken a word since that day. His only reply to any newcomer who condoled with him was to strike himself on his head. It was with much difficulty that Bala persuaded him to eat.

His grief was more shocking to Lalita than even Raju's death. She longed to hear him speak again. Her greatest misfortune now seemed to be this unbridgeable gulf between them. She tried to reach out to him at night, to console him. But he did not even turn to look at her.

That night, Lalita lay awake staring up at the ceiling. She felt him move toward her.

Then finding him sitting beside her, she sat up quickly. Sabhesan held her by the shoulders and suddenly broke down, sobbing. Overwhelmed by pity, Lalita threw her arms round him and drew him closer.

'Come, now...don't weep so!'

'Oh, what have I done! Monstrous sinner that I am...'

Lalita covered his mouth hastily with her hand. 'No, you have not sinned! We are not responsible for things that are beyond us. We are but instruments in His hand...'

'You are trying to assuage my guilt. But I know there can be no redemption for me. Meenu was right. I have murdered him!'

How was she to assuage his guilt?

'Don't torture yourself so. We have to endure the consequences of our past actions—our karma. If it had been ordained that Raju's connection with us should be no more than these ten or twelve years, how could we have changed it?'

Sabhesan lifted his face from her shoulders and drew a little away from her.

'No. I don't deserve this mercy. In the last few days I have realised something else. I know now that you are no ordinary woman. You must be the manifestation of Devi, the Divine mother. I tremble even to look at you. I shudder to think of the way I used to torment you. I dare to come to you only in the dark. I must now ask for your forgiveness...'

'Please don't say such things. I'm just an ordinary woman. All the rest is your imagination.'

'It's no mere fancy. An ordinary woman would have raged like Meenu, given vent to all her spleen.'

'But I'm older. And, should be wiser.'

'But this is no mere wisdom. This is something heavenly.'

She passed her hand softly over his back.

'I'm also a woman, just like any other woman, pining for your love.'

He covered his face with his hands.

'I have never spoken a kind word to you...or to that child. I made him suffer, imagining I was reforming him. All the wealth I accumulated was for him. I thought he would be in difficulties when he grew up.'

Tears welled up in Lalita's eyes. Perhaps this was why Raju was born! To open his father's eyes at last to the truth. What her long penance had failed to achieve, had been achieved by Raju's death!

'Lalita, there's no redemption for me!'

'Don't talk like that! There is no soul that cannot be redeemed by the grace of God!'

'Please, sing that hymn for me – the one from the Tiruppavai, Lalita.'

She laid his head on her lap, and running her fingers through his hair, began to sing, as if singing a lullaby to a child.

Poya pizhaiyum pugu taruvan ninranavam...

'The prayer from a pure heart

Has this power to burn –

To burn our sins of the past

And sins that may still lie in wait for us'

Soon Sabhesan was asleep for the first time in weeks. Carefully, Lalita laid his head on the pillow, and snuggled close to him. Her heart was full. It was as if at last her life had a purpose.

When she woke in the morning, it was past daybreak. Recollections of the night filled her with a sense of joy and fulfillment. But Sabhesan was not there. He must have woken earlier. Quickly she rolled up the mat on which she had slept. When she went to place the rolled mat in its corner, she caught sight of the mirror on the wall. Her face had a big new spot of vermilion on the forehead, and there was a red hibiscus flower in her hair! What did these mean?

Panic gripped her. She went from room to room hurriedly looking for Sabhesan.

But Sabhesan was nowhere to be found.

CHAPTER THIRTY-ONE

'Meenu!'

Meenu woke up with a start. Was that some wounded bird calling?

She heard Lalita's voice again.

'Meenu!' called a doleful voice from the hall.

As Meenu rushed out she could see Lalita holding on to a pillar and sinking down to the floor. The kumkum spot on her forehead was much bigger than usual. And there was a big red hibiscus in her hair!

'Manni, manni!'

Meenu shook her by her shoulders. She had a dazed look.

'Manni, what happened?'

'Your mama is missing. I've looked for him everywhere.'

'Oh, no! Let's look again.'

'I've looked everywhere.'

'Must have left for the fields, then.'

'No, Meenu. He has lost his grip on himself. He has left, I know.'

Bala came hurrying in. On hearing the news she exploded in a torrent of words, 'Oh, this brother of mine! What's he up to now? After all that he's been dishing out all these years, the fellow's gone and deserted you. Now! Now, when you need him most!'

'Mother! Please be quiet! Let's find out if he has gone across to the fields. Let's send word to Pavadai.'

Lalita shook her head.

'You can if you want. But I've no hopes. I ought to have known better. I should have been warned by all he said last night.'

'What did he say?'

'Said he was responsible for Raju's death. He wouldn't be comforted by anything I could say. Went on lamenting that he had no hope of redemption.'

Lakshmi came in a flutter. 'What has happened amma?'

'Go and call Pavadai. We can't find Sami anywhere.'

Lakshmi went out mumbling 'Aiyaiyo! Panaiyatha! What else now? Who knows what else awaits this house!'

Meenu prodded Lalita gently. 'What else did he say?'

'Raju's death seems to have affected him mentally. He said I was Devi's manifestation and he was afraid of me. I was shocked. I told him I was just an ordinary woman—an ordinary woman pining for his love. I don't think he understood.'

'How could this man break our hearts so!' cried Bala.

After a long silence Lalita said, 'The funny thing is, Bala, yesterday, for the first time in my life, he spoke frankly to me and with real warmth. Perhaps he thought that was enough for the rest of my life.'

Meenu wondered if her mama had really left the place. Could he leave his house and his lands—all that he had protected with such fierce possessiveness? He was not like Krishnan who had run away on an impulse. Sabhesan mama had been attached to things—to his puja bowl and spoon as much as to Sankaralinga Iyer's lands. It would not have been in character for him to give up everything just like that, unless he had lost his reason.

If it had all been the result of Raju's death, he must have loved Raju more than she had ever been ready to concede. Lalita manni had been right.

'His heart is not a rock, Meenu. It's weaker than ours.'

Was it Raju's death alone that had shocked him? What about her shouting at him? Had this weak-hearted man trembled at her accusation? As she thought over it, Meenu felt that her words must have intensified his guilt and misery.

Why do things work out as they do?

'Amma!'

Pavadai came into the front corridor. 'I've looked everywhere in the fields, amma. Sami is nowhere.'

'Look for him in the tanks and pools and everywhere, Pavadai.' As Bala said that, her voice broke into a sob.

Lalita said with absolute assurance: 'No, he won't do any such thing, Bala.'

'How can you be sure?'

'Look at me. He has put this kumkum spot on my forehead and this flower in my hair, to show that he won't commit suicide. He knows a widow won't be allowed to wear kumkum and flowers.'

Sheer drama, Meenu muttered to herself. Who'd expect someone like Sabhesan mama to come out with such stuff! Did it mean he cared enough for Lalita manni to save her any further trauma?

'I've sent people all around to look for him, amma.'

The whole street was agog with the news in the next few minutes. People rushed in to find out what had happened. It was not easy to answer all their questions.

'Where could he have gone?'

'Why did he go?'

'How perverse of him!'

Meenu realised with surprise that in spite of all their quarrels, the street was still a single family. These people were engrossed in their own problems, and commented with relish upon their neighbour's problems. But they were still bound by a sense of community, a trace of common humanity.

Hariharan came as soon as he heard the news. 'I'll take my car out and look for him. Please don't worry.'

'Who's that?' asked Bala.

'A lecturer at Meenu's college.'

'Looks like a film star, doesn't he?'

'Depend on my mother to say such a thing at such a moment!' thought Meenu, chagrined.

'Now, the two of you had better get up and brush your teeth. Let's have our coffee. Who knows? Brother may even return while we are drinking our coffee!' said Bala with a healthy practicality.

'Mother's always a realist, manni!'

'That's how one should be. Look at what your mama has done now. He has deserted me as if to demonstrate that nobody lived for anybody else in this world.'

Meenu was shaken. She understood that Lalita had been shocked to the core by Sabhesan's desertion. With difficulty she persuaded her to go up to the well for a wash. It was heart-rending to look at Lalita. This truly wonderful woman, this manni of hers, had known nothing but sorrow all her life. The injustice of it all!

Lalita washed her face and came in. Looking into the wall mirror, she put a bright spot of kumkum on her forehead and smiled at Bala who was peeping at her from the kitchen.

'I know there's no danger to his life, Bala. He won't deceive me.'

How can one describe such thinking, Meenu wondered. Devotion? Womanly virtue? How could she be so attached to a man who had maltreated her so terribly?

'I can't bear your speaking up for that fellow,' said Bala handing her the coffee.

Lalita drank her coffee in silence.

'Please, Mother, say nothing more', whispered Meenu.

A sudden weariness overcame her. The large house now appeared even larger, after the loss of Raju and Sabhesan. She could hear frightening sounds from every corner. How was her manni going to live here alone?

The search conducted by the neighbours and the farm-hands proved fruitless. After a day or two, Hariharan informed the police and had an advertisement put into the newspapers.

The days went by. Nothing was heard of Sabhesan. Meenu sensed her mother's impatience.

'What are you going to do here, all alone, Lalita? Why don't you come with us to Madras?'

'No, Bala. I'd rather be here.'

'All by yourself? Crying all the time, thinking of all that has happened. Not a soul here to comfort you…'

'Being alone is no problem for me. Please don't press me any further, Bala. If he ever feels like coming back, he'll come here. I have to be here and I'm going to be here.'

'You're mad!'

'But he'll come back! I'm sure of it!'

Meenu was surprised to find her mother in tears. 'Oh, the fool that he is! He doesn't know your worth. And he doesn't deserve your love!'

'No, Bala, don't say such things about him. Do you think I'll be pleased to hear you speak like that?'

Meenu found it incredible that Lalita should speak as she did. There never had been a more loving woman – she was like something out of an epic. To love without expectation of return. And such a man! And now Lalita truly grieved for him. Of that Meenu was sure.

Was Meenu herself not partly responsible for this sorrow? How was she to repair the harm done?

'I never thought Sami would do such a thing, Meenu!' She found Lakshmi's concern touching.

'Sami's anger was always extreme. So was his sorrow!' continued Lakshmi.

How true! He was noisily, blusteringly, weak. He did not know how to control his anger or to hide a sense of injury…

'It hurts me to think of our amma's plight, Meenu. She is almost divine. She hasn't known a day's joy in her life. But she continues to smile. Like the Goddess Panaiyatha who stands there smiling for ever in spite of all that's happening in this village!'

This indeed is compassion that embraces the whole world, thought Meenu. It is the love that goes after the lost sheep. Love that can withstand the shocks of life. Yes. It is love that would never stoop to tell her, 'Meenu, he left home because of you!'

Lalita manni's words and actions were not mere wifely virtue. Her love embraced a Rukmini, a Saroji, a Balu Vadyar and a Sankaralinga Iyer, without any distinction.

Meenu stood up.

'How can amma live all alone here, Meenu?' asked Lakshmi. 'Why don't you stay here with her?'

Startled by the question, Meenu just smiled and said, 'I'm going for a walk, Lakshmi. I'll go by myself.'

She soon left the streets behind, and reached the fields.

'Why don't you stay with her?'

Meenu was bewildered. What about her idea of doing her M.A.? And what about all her other plans and dreams for the future – all the things that she had wanted to achieve?

But had she not learnt things here that she could not have learnt in Madras? Had not all the suffering and her manni's smile taught her much? Was she not much clearer in her mind now? Could she find a better guru than her manni?

The green fields before her, the red and yellow butterflies playing hide-and-seek and inviting her to join, the storks hesitating for a moment as if waiting for her to chase them before they flew away—Meenu was arrested by the sight.

'I'll be born as a stork in my next birth!'

He will wait for her here, yearning for a look from her...

'Please stay with us here, Meenu akka, Please. Won't you?'

What did she want another degree for? To widen her knowledge? To help her look for a better job?

As for her ideals and dreams, perhaps they could be fulfilled even here.

How many Rajus are there in this place?

Could she show them the way? Perhaps that was going to be her atonement.

'Meenu!'

She turned back with a smile. How did he manage to be there just then...as if sent for?

'So you're going away, aren't you, Meenu?'

Hariharan was looking at her wistfully.

She laughed softly. 'No, I've decided to stay on.'

His eyes lit up, agreeably surprised. 'Oh, good!' he said.

'I'm going to start a school in Raju's memory. Here, in my mama's house. It would be a school where children would love to learn.'

'Happy news! This would be the best thing that can ever happen to this village. You can count on my co-operation in your project.'

'Thanks.'

'Any news of your mama, Meenu?'

'No.'

'All these happenings must have confirmed you in your belief that the word 'love' signifies nothing...'

She looked straight into his wistful eyes, unable to suppress a surge of affection. 'No, Hariharan. It's only now that I realise what a great force love can be.'

He took her hand in his. 'Any chance you may change your opinion in my case too?'

Withdrawing her hand shyly, she said, 'Please don't hurry me. There have been these terrible tragedies at home. I need time to recover.'

'I'm willing to wait.'

'And I'm quite serious about running that school.'

'I won't stand in your way at all. And I am quite serious about starting that hospital. Manju will be supervising the whole thing.'

'You can count on my cooperation in your project', she said, laughing.

'But I'll ask for more. Nothing less than your companionship—forever.'

'Don't hurry me into anything, please.'

'I'm willing to wait—forever.'

First came the dots. The white spots falling on the wet earth. Blob after blob of chalk powder dropping from Lalita's nimble fingers. She was bent over the ground, drawing the morning kolam at the frontyard. As her hand flew swiftly above, below and around the framework of dots, lotus petals opened out on the ground. Creepers climbed and coiled. And parrots perched on them.

'What a fine artist you are, manni!' said Meenu.

Lalita went on adding a few finishing touches to the parrots feathers. Then she looked up. The kolam patterns kept blooming morning after morning in expectation of Sabhesan's return. As did the calm radiance of Lalita's smile.

Meenu let her eyes traverse the whole street with its row of kolam designs, one in front of each house, drawn on the freshly watered earth. Hariharan, busy dusting his Ambassador, smiled at her. Manju was trying to help him out with his chore, steadying herself on a walker.

She didn't wish to disappoint them. It was just that she felt the need for a little more time...

The children will be here soon, filing into her 'Bal Vihar' and greeting her cheerfully with their 'Vanakkam Meenu akka!'

As they call her 'Meenu akka!' she can hear Raju's voice, poor Raju with his dreams of a home in the heavens.

She turns eagerly to look at the chorusing figures.

Here come Gopu and Venkittu, in their bright dresses. Kitchu, Nanu, Nachami behind them, stepping carefully, without disturbing the kolam...New blooms with new dreams in their eyes...

Glossary

aiya	a respectful form of address for a man
aiyer	brahmin
akka	elder sister
amma	mother; also used for addressing a woman
anna	elder brother
appa	father
cheppan-kizhangu	tubers of Caladium
chettiar	a castename
dabara	small metal bowl used as a saucer
dharma	code of conduct
karma	deeds done in a previous birth whose consequences have to be borne now

kolam	aesthetic designs drawn with rice or chalk powder, every morning, on the patch of ground in front of the houses
kumkum	red powder worn as a spot on the forehead, mostly by women
mama	uncle. Also used to address elderly men
mami	aunt. Also used to address elderly women
manni	elder brother's wife, but the term is used by Meenu to address her aunt
mutt	Hindu monastery
namaskaram	reverential bow; also a term used for greeting people
pancha patra uddharani	metal bowl and spoon used for offering water in religious ceremonies
puja	worship, prayer
sami	respectful form of address for a man
sani	Saturn. Used as a term of abuse
thool-pakoda	spicy fritters made with chick-pea flour
tiffin	light meal, snacks
vedanta	refined system of philosophy. Also used loosely for a philosophical outlook
zamindar	squire, landed gentry

Aadhavan's novel traces the emotional evolution of an adolescent growing into young adulthood. Infatuation, calf love, flirtations, love outside marriage–the yearnings and disappointments that lead to the growth and maturity of a young college student–are the theme of the story. As Ramaseshan is himself the narrator, the reader is privy to his innermost doubts and inferences, not to mention the shifting focus of his attentions. Written with humour and insight, the novel also touches on the gaps between generations trying to understand each other and the slow dawning of clues to complete this exercise successfully.

Bridges is a saga of three generations of upper caste Tamil women. The novel gives the reader rare glimpses into customs and traditions typical of each period it covers—with an unjaundiced eye, great attention to detail, compassion and humour.

The women in *Bridges*—the central figures in the novel—are quite often strong characters. Even the orthodox widow of the early part of the 20th century, with her blind acceptance of hidebound belief systems and rituals, emerges as a personality in her own right, a sense of duty and devotion to family underlying her every action. Each succeeding generation of women is stronger and more emancipated than the previous one.

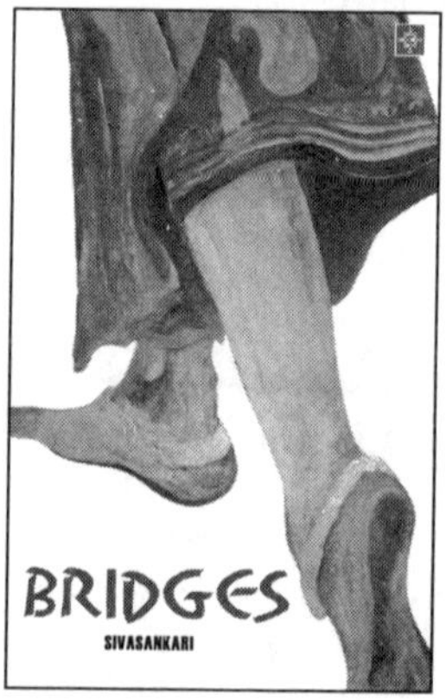

The story spans a time frame of about seven decades and although its women have different life experiences, the leitmotif is the strength that runs through all of them, making each react with courage and dignity to whatever life offers. The men too provide an interesting mix of characters, each a product of his time and milieu. In the process Sivasankari succeeds in capturing the many nuances of the lifestyles of the times.

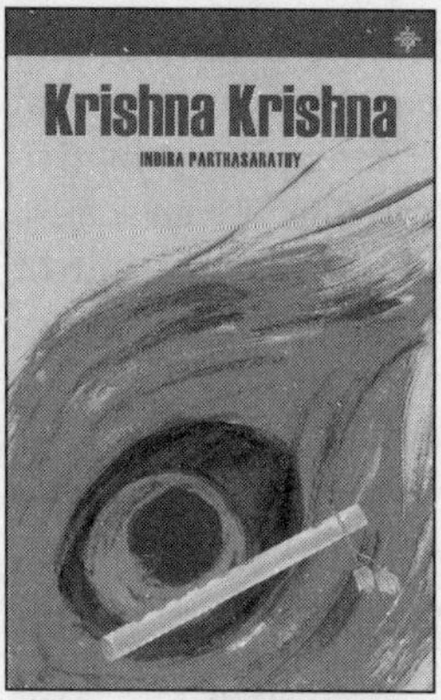

Indira Parthasarathy calls Krishna a metaphor that 'fulfils all the dark and lurking desires in our deep Unconscious and represents the collective vision of the community as a whole.' In his view, Krishna cannot be judged by the 'moral yardstick' set for others either.

Using the pansophical Narada as the narrator widens the scope of the novel and helps contemporize its concerns. Beginning with Jara the hunter shooting an arrow at Krishna's feet in the aftermath of the Kurukshetra war, the author has Narada telling the story of Krishna as revealed to Jara by Krishna. Indira Parthasarathy's Krishna is not only an amalgam of the Harivamsam, Sri Bhagavatam, Vishnu Purana and the Mahabharata but the vehicle that carries their cultural and aesthetic themes into a literary discussion of the idea of Krishna

---

Wings in the Void gives the reader a peep into the Delhi of the1960s, a city suffering the bitter after-taste of the sweet victory of Independence. The Mahatma's ideals have been finally buried; corruption, venality and platitudes rule, not only the capital's corridors of power, but also the lives of the individuals who live in it.

Among the most significant of Indira Parthasarathy's novels, *Wings in the Void* explores the wheeling and dealing, ambition and greed that rule the lives of countless upwardly mobile Indians caught up in the intrigues of the political and diplomatic circles of Delhi. Into this complex world arrives Kasturi, a young intellectual in the making from a small town in Tamil Nadu, in search of wealth, success and personal freedom. The novel is an account of his mental and emotional evolution. What Kasturi achieves-and loses in the process-mirrors the experiences of many young modern urban Indians in their struggle for a better life.

Once an Actress is about an intense interplay of emotions in a relationship punctuated by intolerance, separation and eventual reunion. An essentially cerebral columnist, Ranga is a sensitive person struggling to overcome his feudal upbringing. For an actress brought up on mainstream theatre, Kalyani is a connoisseur of arts of uncommon maturity. Ranga adores Kalyani but seeks constant evidence of her love for him. Kalyani finds her life's meaning in her involvement with Ranga. Love for her is sincerity, honesty and compassion, not its overt demonstration. This unsettles Ranga. A helpless victim of his chauvinistic pettiness with its thin veneer of intellectual gloss, Ranga seeks and obtains separation from Kalyani. The eventual reunion with a now disabled Kalyani is a moving denouement.

Kalyani is perhaps the most sensitive woman character created by Jayakanthan. The novel offers rare insights into the inner reaches of the human mind. It is a perceptive portrayal of the low-intensity conflict between a sentimental man and a self-sufficient woman.

Jayakanthan's novel, *Love and Loss,* is a sensitive 'slice of life' story that explores the lives of Thangam, a construction worker and her son Chitti, born out of wedlock. The squalid slums of erstwhile Madras, now Chennai, form the grimy background to the tender drama of a woman trying to find an anchor to her life in a roadside astrologer she befriends, and the furious resentment and protest this engenders in her son.

Originally titled *Unnaipol Oruvan* in Tamil, it portrays a milieu that was not often the stuff of fiction in the 1960s. It was made into an award-winning film.

Star-Crossed is a novel about the world of Tamil cinema minus the glamour. It takes a keen look at the lives of film-makers, technicians, producers and actors. Turning the spotlight on the fringes of the entertainment world, Ashokamitran exposes the daily trials and tribulations of a cast of characters none too familiar to those who equate the world of celluloid with the proverbial dream factory.

The original Tamil title, *Karainda Nizhalgal*, conveys the tragedy and uncertainty inherent in the lives of these providers of mass entertainment, whose fortunes rise and fall or sink altogether with the making of a film. Simply told, the tale reveals the nitty-gritty of the ordinary lives in the shadows that collaborate to create magic for the silver screen. Told in simple, unsentimental language, the story is nonetheless profoundly moving.